It didn't matter how attractive Vicky was...

Or any other woman, for that matter. It didn't matter how good it felt to have her hand wrapped around his arm, knowing that the contact was giving her the support she needed. It didn't matter that he could smell the hint of flowers and musk drifting from her skin, or that her long blond hair was like spun gold against the dark fabric of his suit. It didn't matter that the last hour had made him feel more alive than he had in several years and that he was actually looking forward to sharing a meal with her.

As the common idiom went, he'd been there and done that already, and had the scars on his heart to prove it.

Dear Reader,

A while ago I was lucky enough to spend a week in Cumbria, in the northwest of England. As I was revisiting places I first came to know when our children were small, I found I was looking at them in a completely different way.

Suddenly, the quaint little market town of years ago was growing and becoming the background for a whole new cast of characters working in and around Denison Memorial Hospital. This book is the third in a series of stories about those characters, and I hope you enjoy them.

Perhaps along the way I can give you a taste of what it was like to live surrounded by such magnificent scenery and the inimitable Cumbrian people. I will certainly be going back again.

Happy reading!

Josie

Innocent Secret

Josie Metcalfe

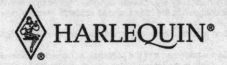

TORONTO • NEW YORK • LONDON
AMSTERDAM • PARIS • SYDNEY • HAMBURG
STOCKHOLM • ATHENS • TOKYO • MILAN • MADRID
PRAGUE • WARSAW • BUDAPEST • AUCKLAND

ISBN 0-373-06355-5

INNOCENT SECRET

First North American Publication 2002

Printed in U.S.A.

CHAPTER ONE

'DO YOU take this man to be your lawful wedded husband?'

Vicky Lawrence heard the time-honoured words drifting towards her, and with them knew that a dream that she'd treasured for nearly half of her life was finally over.

She'd loved Nick ever since she was twelve years old but he'd never looked at her the way he was looking at Frankie, the woman who was making her promises to him.

She didn't begrudge him his happiness—how could she when the two of them looked as if they'd been made for each other?

Still, she wouldn't be human if she didn't feel a pang of regret for what might have been. She'd believed all her Christmases had come at once the day he'd proposed to her, and the months when she'd been busily planning their perfect wedding had been the happiest of her life.

She still didn't know what had changed, or why, or even when. All she did know was that when Nick had sat her down with that serious look on his face and confessed that he wanted to break their engagement, she couldn't have been more delighted.

It should have hurt to find out that he'd fallen passionately in love with a fellow GP working in the unit that was part of Denison Memorial Hospital. The fact

5

that she knew and liked Frankie as a colleague should have made her feel betrayal, not gratitude.

Yet here she was, standing surreptitiously at the back of the room so that her presence wouldn't cast a shadow over the proceedings, and she hardly felt a qualm.

She'd searched around inside her heart, almost like probing at a painful tooth with her tongue, and had barely raised an ache, but if she'd admitted as much to any of the people in the room they wouldn't have believed her.

'Are you all right?' had been the most frequent question she'd heard over the last few weeks, accompanied by a look of such cloying pity that she'd wanted to scream.

'I'm fine,' she'd been saying with a bright smile when what she'd wanted to say had been, 'I couldn't be more delighted that Nick fell in love with Frankie because it saved me from making a monumental mistake.'

However, the world and his wife had cast her in the role of broken-hearted waif and wouldn't look beyond to see that there was something far more important than Nick's defection filling her mind.

'Are you all right?' murmured yet another voice as someone came to stand just behind her, and the soft burr of his Scottish accent told her who it was without needing to see him.

This time her reaction to the question was very different. This time the voice was the one that, over the last couple of months, had begun to fill her mind and heart with more desperate longing than she'd ever felt for Nick. She hadn't realised that she'd had little more than an adolescent crush on her long-time hero until she'd learned about the real thing. There was no comparison.

'I'm fine,' she whispered over her shoulder, looking up almost six inches into the sombre, handsome face of GP Joe Faraday and straight into the changeable hazel of his eyes. It was her usual reply, honed over the last roller-coaster weeks and, as usual, she could tell that she hadn't been believed.

Sometimes she didn't even believe it herself. It wasn't quite as easy as that to let go of something that had been the bedrock of her existence for half her life.

She took another long look at the handsome man now slipping a wedding ring on the finger of his petite new wife. She'd dreamed of him doing that to her one day, but he'd never have worn that same look of utter devotion as he did with Frankie, neither would he have thrown a cheerful smile of resignation at ten-year-old Katie's whispered interruption.

She sighed, knowing that Nick was doing the right thing, knowing that they had *both* made the right decision.

Not that any amount of certainty was going to make the next few weeks any easier to bear. That was one of the penalties of living in such a place as Edenthwaite. It was a caring community with most of its members connected by blood or work, but that also meant that the world and his wife had heard at least one version of the story currently going the rounds.

Unfortunately, most of them were determined to see her in the role of jilted bride-to-be and were treating her as if she'd suddenly turned into eggshell porcelain.

Wondering just how long it would be before life

returned to normal, she sighed again and was startled to feel the warm weight of a decidedly masculine arm encompass her shoulders.

'We don't have to stay,' Joe murmured, his voice a deep rumble close to her ear that sent a sharp shiver of awareness right through her.

For a moment Vicky was lost in the sensation of quiet strength and concern, then the irony of the situation washed over her. This was Dr Joseph Faraday standing with his arm around her, the most reclusive man she'd ever met. Over the six months or so since she'd started work at Denison Memorial she didn't think he'd glanced in her direction more than half a dozen times, even when they'd been on the ward together, and as for speaking... Even when she'd gone out of her way to help him in the aftermath of his injury it had been rather like dealing with a grumpy hedgehog.

'*We* don't have to?' Had she heard right?

'The invitation to the reception *was* informal,' he reminded her. 'If you'd prefer, we could have a meal somewhere other than Edenthwaite.'

For a moment Vicky was tempted, so very tempted. She'd been waiting for months for the man to notice her...*really* notice her. She'd never expected that the distance Joe maintained between himself and the rest of the world would be breached by her own apparent misfortune. And the informality of today's celebrations *was* deliberate so that friends and fellow members of staff would be able to slot in their attendance around shift times.

'I can't,' she murmured, hoping her frustration wasn't too evident. She'd been trying to find a way through the barbed wire of Joe's defences for so long

and now she was going to have to turn him down. Or
was she?

'It was just a suggestion,' he began, starting to
withdraw, but she turned impetuously towards him,
catching hold of his suit sleeve to stop him turning
away.

'Joe, don't you see? I *have* to go, otherwise the
gossips will have even more to talk about. But I don't
have to stay long.'

She had that prickly feeling that she was being
watched. Past his broad shoulder she caught sight of
several interested faces turned in their direction and
wanted to groan. It wasn't her imagination. Everyone
seemed to be watching her every move. It felt almost
as if she were living in a goldfish bowl.

'Just long enough to show your face?' he asked
quietly, his expression somewhere between wary and
understanding.

She nodded.

'And then you can escape with a clear conscience?'

She nodded again and was gifted with a glimpse
of a surprisingly mischievous smile.

'In that case, let's hope it's a very short reception
line,' he muttered with a quick glower at two of the
more inquisitive ladies sitting in front of them.

Vicky knew that their hushed conversation
wouldn't have carried to the pair—she and Joe were
far too aware of the perils of unwary conversations to
risk it. However, she had noticed that the pair seemed
to have spent almost more time looking back at her
and her companion than they had at Frankie and Nick.

Hopefully, they hadn't been watching when he'd
put his comforting arm around her shoulders. That

was an unexpectedly sweet memory which she didn't want tainted by any gossip.

'I now pronounce you man and wife,' the registrar declared, the words breaking through her scrambled thoughts. Even though she knew everything had changed for the best, she'd been dreading this moment and found herself staring with an awful sort of fascination as Nick turned to Frankie and took her in his arms.

So eager, she thought with a strange little ache around her heart. He obviously didn't need anyone to tell him that he could now kiss his new bride, and with such passion, too. When it had been *her,* he'd barely done more than brush her lips with his.

What would it be like to be kissed like that? To have a man pour his heart and soul into—?

'Vicky?' The deep voice at her elbow was accompanied by a gentle hand at her cheek, turning her to face him. His hazel eyes were dark with sympathy. 'You don't have to watch,' he said softly. 'No one would have blamed you if you hadn't come at all. You could have made certain you were on duty instead.'

His gentle concern was like a balm to her spirits, reminding her that he didn't know the real reason why she'd been willing to release Nick from his promise. Very few people did. Even Nick didn't know the full story. To ease his conscience she'd had to tell him that she was falling in love with someone else, but had deliberately withheld the name of the man. That was something only *she* knew.

'No, I couldn't have stayed away,' she said softly as bride and groom walked past them on their way out, closely followed by two ecstatic bridesmaids. 'If

I hadn't come, it might have cast a shadow over their day, with people wondering where I was and if I was nursing a broken heart.'

'So here you are with all flags flying, daring the gossips to do their worst.'

'Not quite,' she admitted with a shudder as they waited their turn to leave, grateful for the happy buzz of conversation that left them free to talk more easily. 'It was bad enough when everyone was cooing over our engagement and wanting updates on the wedding preparations. To be honest, I'm dreading the reception.'

'Not any more. Remember? We're only staying long enough to say our congratulations and then we're out of there.'

He took her hand and looped it over his arm in an almost courtly way as he ushered her out of the door. The sudden lift that the gesture gave to her spirits was something she hadn't expected. It was almost as if he was making himself her escort…her protector.

'This way, please,' called a voice, and they turned simultaneously to find themselves caught in the flash of a photographer. 'Lovely! Thank you,' the young man called, and turned as if to pursue his next quarry.

Although the weather was dry and bright, March in Cumbria was still far too cold for a lengthy posing session and within ten minutes they were all on their way to the nearby hotel where the reception was being held.

Joe wasn't happy.

There were far too many people in here for his liking, and as for the volume of noise… What it would be like by the time everyone had a drink or two inside them didn't bear thinking about.

Over the last few years he'd grown accustomed to dealing with humanity on a one-to-one basis. The largest concentration was the shifting numbers of colleagues he might find in the staff lounge at the start of the day.

Joe was seriously tempted to cut and run but then the small hand she'd placed on his arm tightened its grip slightly—almost as if Vicky knew what he was contemplating—and he knew he couldn't do that to her.

He knew she wasn't really his responsibility. She was a native of the area after all, and should have plenty of family and friends who could keep her company.

Except she'd seemed determined to go through it alone.

He'd only intended sticking his nose through the door to say he'd been to the ceremony, but when he'd seen her standing all alone at the back of the room, so valiant in her solitude, something had prompted him to approach her.

It had been an uncharacteristic thing for him to do—he hadn't been dubbed 'that Scots recluse' without cause—but there had been something about the stiff way she'd been holding her slender shoulders that told him she was suffering, and if there was one thing he understood…

Not that it was a hardship to spend time in her company. It wasn't.

Vicky Lawrence was a bright, beautiful young woman with a natural inclination towards caring for people. It wasn't even restricted to her nursing either.

He'd been quite surprised by the way she'd insisted on spending time with him in the immediate aftermath of his recent shoulder injury.

Granted, the dislocation had caused a fair degree of trauma to the joint and the residual bruising was still restricting the range of movement. At first he'd believed that it had just been the fact that she'd been the first on the scene after the accident had happened that had sparked her interest. But that didn't explain why she had still been volunteering to take over the more awkward household chores several days later.

There had been something far too intimate about the thought of beautiful young Vicky changing the sheets on his bed or sorting his laundry. He'd been relieved to tell her that his cleaner took care of those tasks, but he hadn't been able to dissuade her from collecting his shopping or providing him with a fresh sling at intervals no matter how grumpy he'd been.

Now *she* needed a little support, although in her case it was emotional rather than practical. Still, if he looked on this interlude as some form of payback, it should make his penance easier to bear—that, and the prospect of leaving for a quiet meal as soon as they'd said their piece. It shouldn't take long and the prospect of spending an hour or so in her company was something he could even look forward to.

Joe helped her out of her coat and folded it over his arm in preparation for a quick getaway then surprised himself by noticing the quiet elegance of the dark sapphire dress she wore. He wasn't usually aware of women's fashions but couldn't help but see the way the fabric draped fluidly over her slender body, accentuating both her height and the unexpectedly mature curves usually hidden by her uniform.

What on earth was he doing? Ogling the poor girl when he was supposed to be keeping her company at a traumatic time? He dragged his eyes away to scan the room rapidly filling with smiling family and friends. Several were looking questioningly at the two of them standing together and that dratted photographer was already at it again, seemingly more fascinated with Vicky than the new bride. Still, he hoped no one had witnessed his lapse.

Not that fellow GP Jack Lawrence was looking any too pleased to see his little sister in his company, but divided loyalties would keep him out of their hair. As best man to his long-time friend Nick he would have little opportunity to take care of Vicky himself.

Anyway, it was only for one afternoon. He could bear the inquisitive glances and the whispers, knowing that they would soon be over.

What he wasn't quite so sure of was whether he would want this enforced closeness to end.

There was something unexpectedly pleasant about being part of a couple again, even if it was just a temporary thing and just for appearances' sake. It certainly couldn't be anything more than that. The girl must be almost young enough to be his daughter, for heaven's sake. What was she...twenty-one? Twenty-two? Impossibly young when compared to his own thirty-seven, even if he had been interested in any sort of a relationship.

No, today he would act as a buffer for her, and then tomorrow would be back to normal. He'd had his chance at happy-ever-after and for a while it had been everything he could have wished. He was resigned to his solitude now, no matter how much his body might appreciate Vicky's charms.

'Ready?' he murmured with a slightly gruff edge to his voice. He was surprised and strangely pleased when she immediately took hold of his arm again, her hand feeling somehow *right* as it curved around the muscles of his forearm.

He heard her draw in a deep breath and blow it out in a steady stream, as though steadying herself for the ordeal ahead, then she looked up to meet his eyes.

'Ready,' she agreed with a determined nod and a tightening of her grip, and they set off towards the small group clustered around the newly-weds.

'Congratulations, Nick,' Joe said, shaking the man's hand. He was determined to ignore the little voice that wondered whether *he'd* looked that happy on *his* wedding day.

'I hope you'll both be very happy,' Vicky added with every semblance of meaning the words.

Joe found himself watching her closely as she spoke to Frankie for a moment, wondering if she was just very good at putting on a front. To his surprise, he couldn't tell. Surely she should have been showing *some* animosity towards the woman who had stolen her fiancé's affections? As far as he could tell, she seemed to genuinely like the other woman and really wished her well.

Surely she wasn't that shallow? This was the girl who had pined after her older brother's best friend for at least a dozen years, culminating in their fairy-tale engagement just a few months ago. Could she really switch off her feelings so quickly? Was she the sort of person who no longer wanted something once she had it in her grasp?

He didn't like to think so, not when she'd been the

only one to awaken the protective instincts that had lain dormant since he'd lost Celia.

Vicky turned to speak to Nick, and Joe thought he might have part of his answer. She was smiling and chatting with the ease of an old friend, but only he knew that her hand had tightened like a tourniquet around his arm.

He covered the slender fingers with his own, hiding the tension-whitened knuckles from view. Unfortunately Nick noticed and there was wary speculation in the glance that went from one face to the other and back to their joined hands.

Joe could hardly snatch his hand away, neither was this the time or the place to make explanations. All he could do was look the man in the eye and dare him to make anything of it. Only time would show that this was just a performance he and Vicky were putting on for the occasion.

Except...

There was something in Nick's expression that gave him a jolt. Something that looked almost like approval when he looked from one to the other of them. Something that made Joe suddenly desperate to retreat as far and as fast as he could into the confines of his own safe world.

He wasn't interested in a relationship, and that was the end of the matter.

It didn't matter how attractive Vicky was—or any other woman for that matter. It didn't matter how good it felt to have her hand wrapped around his arm, knowing that the contact was giving her the support she needed. It didn't matter that he could smell the hint of flowers and musk drifting from her skin or that her long blonde hair was like spun gold against the dark fabric of his suit. It didn't matter that the last hour had made him feel more alive than he had in several years and that he was actually looking forward to sharing a meal with her.

As the common idiom went, he'd been there and done that already, and had the scars on his heart to prove it.

He was just about to make their excuses when Frankie grabbed Nick's arm, her face suddenly pale and clammy as she hurried towards the nearest bathroom.

'Oops! Sorry, folks,' Nick said with a slightly strained chuckle before he followed her. 'Graphic illustration of the fact that morning sickness isn't confined to mornings.'

The realisation that Frankie was already pregnant brought the swift stab of painful memories and Vicky's hastily smothered gasp told Joe that she hadn't known about the pregnancy either.

At least the spreading ripple of understanding laughter meant that people had overheard Nick's devious way of announcing his impending fatherhood. That should take people's minds off the fact that he and Vicky were leaving so soon.

'I think that's our signal to fade into the woodwork,' he suggested quietly, but she didn't say a word.

He escorted her towards the door, wondering why she suddenly felt so fragile beside him, and had to glare at the overzealous photographer when he wanted to take yet another picture of Vicky. She certainly wasn't in the mood to have a camera pointed in her direction and Joe actually had the strange impression that if he moved too fast she might shatter into a thousand fragments.

Her movements were quite wooden as he helped her into her coat and she was moving almost like a sleepwalker as he ushered her out of the hotel and into his car.

He waited for her to fasten her seat belt but she just sat in the dark silence of the car, staring blindly out of the windscreen.

'Vicky?' he prompted. 'Seat belt?'

'Hmm?' The expression she turned on him was somehow dazed and he had to repeat the reminder before she began to fumble her compliance.

'Let me,' he offered, speaking softly and moving slowly to take the catch from her, feeling as if he were dealing with an injured animal.

He wanted to take her hands in his and try to persuade her to talk about what had brought this on, but now was neither the time nor the place.

Knowing that any one of the people they'd just left could emerge from the hotel to see them sitting together in his car, he started the engine and set off out of the car park.

Obviously they were going to have to abandon the idea of going out for a meal. Vicky wasn't in any fit state to cope with the niceties of public dining. The only option was to take her home, but whose?

It wasn't far to the place where he'd had his painful run-in with the escaped bullocks and, just past it, the fork in the road that demanded a decision.

One way led to the renovated farm labourer's cottage she'd told him about when she'd been trying to distract him from the pain of his dislocated shoulder;

the other led to the small stone-built farmhouse which was more a refuge than a home to him.

The thought of inviting anyone into his safe haven made him uncomfortable, but the thought of delivering Vicky to a solitary evening felt equally wrong.

Anyway, he temporised as he accelerated away from her turning, she needed to eat and he had no idea what she'd have in her kitchen. At least he knew his fridge could supply the essentials, thanks to Vicky's persistence. And there was a wry, pleasing irony that he would be feeding her with the food she'd chosen and bought for him.

'We're here, Vicky,' he said as he pulled into the small enclosed yard to one side of the house.

He wasn't surprised when she didn't comment but his understanding turned to concern when she didn't react when he opened the door beside her.

The harsh brilliance of the safety light, activated by their arrival, flooded the interior of the car and painted its silent inmate with unforgiving accuracy.

She looked as perfect as a marble statue, but when had marble statues ever had silvery tears trickling down their cheeks?

'Come on, Vicky. Out you get,' he encouraged as he reached across her to release her seat belt. He had to stretch his shoulder some way beyond what was comfortable to reach it, but that hardly mattered when Vicky was in such misery.

She didn't even seem to realise that she was crying as he let them into the house through the back door which took them straight into the kitchen.

It wasn't the first time that he'd been grateful for the enveloping warmth of the Aga cooker. He didn't even bother taking her coat off as he grabbed a chair and settled her in it as close as possible to the warmth.

For just a moment he stood there looking at her, feeling completely at a loss.

He hardly knew the woman, for heaven's sake. What on earth was he supposed to do or say to help her, to bring her out of this?

'Tea,' he muttered, reaching for the kettle and putting it on the hob to boil. 'If in doubt make a pot of tea.'

He was out of his depth here, and didn't mind admitting it. The psychiatry he'd learned during his training was enough to tell him that Vicky's mental state was no steadier than her physical one. All he could think to do was bury himself in the familiar ritual of pouring milk into the waiting mugs while he waited for the tea to steep.

Did she take sugar? He didn't even know her well enough for that small detail, had never bothered to notice such a thing when they'd been in the same room. Whether she did or not, she was having some. She was borderline shocky and the sugar boost would give her body something to fight with.

'Here.' He crouched beside her chair and wrapped her icy hand around the chunky handle. 'It's hot, but see if you can sip it.'

She barely acknowledged him and the way those silent tears continued to slide down her cheeks, one after another, caused something unfamiliar to tighten inside his chest.

'Please, Vicky.' Joe reached up to cup one damp cheek in his hand and turned her to face him. 'Please, drink some of the tea. You need it.'

As though waking from a nightmare, she focused

on his face and blinked, almost as if surprised to see
him there.

'Joe?'

He'd never heard her voice sounding so lost and
alone. He might not join in with the banter that usually characterised any gathering of staff at Denison
Memorial, but he couldn't help having noticed that
this strikingly beautiful young woman had a bright
bubbly personality to match. It almost hurt to see her
looking so…so defeated.

'Drink,' he urged, cupping one hand around hers
where she held the steaming mug in a white-knuckled
grip and lifting it towards her mouth.

'Don't.' With a shake of her head she resisted, her
brows drawing into a frown as she tried to pass the
mug to him. 'I don't need that. I need to know…'

She had to pause when her lips began to quiver
uncontrollably. He saw her press them firmly together
and heard the deep breath she drew and held as she
fought for control.

'What do you need?' he asked gently. 'Is it something I can get for you? Something to eat?' He wasn't
a brilliant cook but anything short of cordon bleu and
he'd give it a go if it would take that expression out
of her eyes.

She shook her head. 'Oh, Joe, it's nothing like
that,' she said with a hitch in her voice. 'I just need
to know why.'

'Why?' And he'd thought he'd been all at sea before. She'd completely lost him now. 'You mean,
why did Nick marry Frankie? But you know—'

'Not that,' she broke in almost impatiently. 'I know
he married her because they fell in love. Because he
loved her more than he ever loved me…'

'Ah, Vicky, don't do this to yourself,' he begged, feeling panic-induced sweat prickling between his shoulder-blades.

He *really* didn't want to be having this conversation. What did *he* know about what she was going through? He and Celia had met in their teens and there had never been anyone else for either of them, right up to the day she'd died.

'No, Joe, I need to know,' she insisted with a spark of her former energy. 'I know we both did the right thing to call off our wedding and I really hope they're happy but...but I need to know what's wrong with me.'

'Wrong with you?' he said, more lost than ever. Would he ever unravel the Gordian knot of a woman's thought processes? 'But there's *nothing* wrong with you.'

'There must be,' she said adamantly, with a sad droop to a mouth now bare of any lipstick. 'Otherwise *I'd* be the one expecting his baby rather than Frankie.'

'You...' He gave up. Did she want to be pregnant? Surely not, without a marriage in her near future. With her engagement so recently broken she wouldn't even have a close relationship to rely on.

'He's only known Frankie for a matter of *weeks,* Joe,' she barrelled on suddenly, as though the words and the emotions behind them wouldn't be contained any longer. 'They're married now, but they obviously didn't bother to wait before they went to bed because she's already expecting his baby. So what was wrong with *me*? He was engaged to me for nearly six months and he never gave me anything more than a kiss and a hug.'

CHAPTER TWO

Two days later Vicky still couldn't believe what she'd said, and to have said it to Joe!

Just thinking about the embarrassment of it made her go hot and cold, but at the time her thought processes had been so scrambled that she'd had no idea that she was going to make such a momentous revelation.

She groaned silently, her thoughts still scurrying around in her head in spite of the fact that she'd been trying to keep busy to switch the thoughts off. As if it wasn't bad enough that she must be the only twenty-six-year-old virgin in Edenthwaite, she had to go and tell Joe, the one man whose opinion of her really mattered.

How was she going to face him again? It had been difficult enough putting up with all the sympathetic murmurs of her colleagues when they'd found out about Nick and Frankie. If they discovered that her adolescent crush on Nick had prevented her from indulging in the flings her colleagues seemed to flit in and out of, she'd probably never live it down.

Could she trust Joe not to say anything?

She could hardly bring herself to think about it, let alone hold a conversation begging for his discretion.

'Vicky. Phone call for you,' called one of the juniors, beckoning her from the other side of the ward, and she hurried across to the desk. There were several sets of lab results she'd been chasing up ever since she'd come on duty and they'd promised to phone them through as soon as they were ready.

'Hello. Vicky Lawrence speaking,' she said crisply, but when she waited for a reply all she could hear was the faint crackle of an open line. 'Hello? Is there anyone there?'

When there was still no answer she shrugged and put the phone down. 'Who was it, Sue? Did they say what they wanted?'

'Sorry, Vicky.' Sue shook her head. 'It was a man and he wanted to speak to you. I don't know any more than that.'

'A man?' The person she was waiting to speak to was definitely not a man, so perhaps it hadn't been the lab results. 'Oh, well. They'll just have to try again.'

'They will, if it's important,' Sue agreed. 'Let's hope it isn't anything complicated and that they don't phone back in the middle of the patients' lunch.'

Vicky groaned. It wasn't often that they had so many who needed individual help with their meals, but the last few days had been dreadful. For some reason there had been an overflow from the geriatric ward into her general one. Now she was trying to cope with one gentleman who was flat on his back with both legs in traction and a woman in her sixties whose years of a strict vegan diet had left her with multiple fractures in a collapsed spine, rendering her all but immobile.

Apart from them, there was a man in his late fifties who had been born with Down's syndrome. Although Owen was physically capable of feeding himself, he still required constant supervision if the food was actually going to be consumed while it was hot. At least his broken leg was keeping him in one place at the moment. His elderly carers had warned that once he was mobile again he was quite likely to go wandering off at any time.

'And won't that be just what I need to brighten my day,' Vicky muttered as she tried to juggle the number of patients requiring individual attention against the staff available for the task. 'And some time during all that, the staff have to go for their lunch-breaks, too!'

Her calculations were interrupted by the phone and she reached out to lift the receiver without taking her eyes off her little chart.

'Hello. Sister Lawrence, General Ward,' she said automatically, more than half of her mind on possible permutations that would get the job done. Would she need to ring around for some temporary help, just until the older patients were able to move into their proper domain?

It was several seconds before she realised that no one had spoken since she'd answered the phone.

'Hello?' she prompted, but once again there was just that faint crackle of an open line. 'Is there someone there?'

Although there wasn't a sound from the other end, for some reason she just knew that there was someone there, someone listening to her.

The hairs on the back of her neck felt as if they were standing on end, almost as if a cold draught had blown across her, but she knew that was nonsense in a modern building like this.

'I'm sorry, but I haven't got time to waste,' she said, firmly squashing the sneaking feeling of unease.

'If you're not going to speak I'll have to put the phone down.'

She started counting silently, determined to carry out her threat on the count of five. She'd only got as far as four when she heard a single whispered word before the connection was abruptly broken.

She was sitting there, staring at the receiver still clasped in her shaking hand, when a familiar baritone voice nearly had her jumping out of her skin.

'Vicky? What on earth's wrong with you?' Joe demanded when she'd shrieked and dropped the phone. He picked it up from the floor and put it to his ear before he deposited it where it belonged.

Whether he was checking to see if there was someone still on the line or whether the thing was still working, she didn't know.

She was trembling all over now, and it wasn't because Joe had startled her.

'Are you all right?' he demanded, so she knew she must be looking as shaky as she felt. 'Is there something I can do or would you rather I came back later?'

'No!' she said hurriedly, suddenly far more worried that he might leave than that his presence might be an embarrassment. She'd been dreading this first meeting, after her blurted revelation, but that phone call had really given her the creeps. 'No, Joe, please, don't go.'

'What's the matter? Aren't you feeling well?' He perched one hip on the corner of the desk, bringing those changeable hazel eyes almost down to her level. The clear concern in them was like a balm to her jangling nerves.

'I'm all right, except...except for that weird phone call. And I don't think it was the first one.' Now that she thought about it, there had been something similar yesterday, too.

'Weird? How was it weird? Who was calling?'

'I don't know who it was.'

'So, what did they want?' He was patience itself but that didn't do anything for her agitation.

'I don't know what he wanted,' she retorted snappishly. 'The first couple of times he didn't say anything at all but this time—'

'Whoa! What do you mean, the first couple of times?' he interrupted sharply. 'What's going on here? It can hardly be a disappointed suitor—there hasn't been time since your engagement to Nick. Wait a minute! You're not telling me you're being stalked, are you? How long has this been going on?'

'No! Of course I'm not being stalked,' she countered dismissively, then paused, feeling sick.

It was crazy to even think about it in a place like Edenthwaite, but suddenly she found herself wondering if the idea made sense. Had there been too many 'silent' calls over the last few days for it to be an accident?

'Oh, Joe, I don't know,' she admitted in a small voice. 'Perhaps I am.'

'Hey, Vicky, take it easy.' He reached for her hand, and when he tucked it warmly and firmly between his she suddenly had the crazy feeling that Joe was going to keep her safe. 'Now, take a deep breath and tell me what's been going on.'

'There hasn't really been anything going on except for a few phone calls, and they could have been anything. I didn't even know it was a man calling until this last time, when he spoke.'

'So, where were the calls coming from? Inside the

hospital through the internal switchboard or from out-side? What was the reception like? Could the caller have been using a mobile perhaps? And his voice—did you recognise it? Did it sound local or did it have a different accent?'

'He only said one word. My name.' She shuddered at the memory of the strangely menacing whisper, or was her imagination working overtime to make it sound menacing?

'Your name?' he prompted keenly. 'Did he say Vicky or Sister Lawrence?'

'Neither. He said Victoria. And could you let me answer one set of questions before you ask another? Were you Sherlock Holmes in another life?'

He chuckled ruefully and gave her hands a squeeze. 'Sorry, but one idea leads to another. Can you re-member what you said when you answered the phone? Did you give the caller your name, or just the name of the ward?'

The way he'd kept hold of her hand and the gentle smile that softened the usual sombreness of his face made her feel warm inside, but Vicky fought off the distraction to replay that last phone call in her mind.

'I think it was an outside line,' she said slowly, mentally sorting through her impressions. 'There was a sort of hollow crackle that you don't get with the hospital lines, so I would automatically say, "Sister Lawrence, General Ward."'

'And he said…?'

'Nothing at first. It was only when I told the caller that I was too busy to waste time and I was going to put the phone down that he spoke, and then *he* hung up.'

'And the other times?'

'I hadn't really noticed them,' she confessed. 'It was only *this* time that made me realise that the other "nobody there" phone calls could have been from the same person.'

'Did he say anything else or make any noises?'

'Just my name,' she said with a renewed shiver.

'And how did he say it? What tone of voice did he use? Was it normal volume or whispered?'

'Not exactly a whisper, more like…Vic*to*ria.' She tried to give it exactly the same stress that *he* had, in the same singsong way. 'But I didn't recognise his voice and I couldn't really say whether he had a local accent or not.'

Those changeable hazel eyes of Joe's were dark with concentration and she could tell that he was going over everything she had told him. She knew it was stupid but she really wanted him to be able work it all out, to be able to come up with a simple answer to what was going on.

'Has anyone else taken one of these calls for you?' he asked suddenly, his gaze almost too analytical for comfort.

'Anyone else?' She frowned as she tried to work out the significance of the question. When it struck her she was devastated at the implication and dragged her hand away from him to leap up from her seat. She refused to let herself dwell on the pang of loss she felt when the contact was broken between them. What was the point of physical contact when there was suspicion between them?

'You mean, can anyone corroborate my story or am I making the whole thing up?' she glared down at him, lounging so nonchalantly on the corner of the desk as though he hadn't just accused her of fabricating a stupid lie. What on earth would be the point? It wasn't as if she lacked a social life, in spite of the fact that her wedding hadn't taken place. 'Do you think I'm inventing it to get the sympathy vote now that I've been left on the shelf? What kind of misfit do you think I am?'

'Calm down, Vicky,' Joe ordered, grabbing for her hand as she stomped past him for the second time, trying to control her rising temper by striding up and down in the restricted space. 'That's not what I meant at all. I was only wondering if he'd said more than your name so another person might have picked up on an accent or something.'

'Oh.' She hung her head and blew out an exasperated breath while she gathered up the courage to meet his gaze. 'I'm sorry, Joe. That was unfair of me, especially when you're only trying to help. It's all probably a lot of fuss about absolutely nothing but…but I've got to admit it's got me a bit spooked.'

'With good reason. By all accounts this sort of thing is happening far too frequently these days. The statistics probably don't show the full extent of the problem because most women are afraid to say anything for fear of being ridiculed.'

'And then I turn on you,' she said apologetically. 'Will you forgive me?'

'Of course. Or should I say, provided you promise to let me know if it happens again?'

Vicky's independent streak made her want to insist that she could deal with the problem herself, and that if the incidents didn't escalate from the present level, she would probably be able to. But that wasn't what Joe wanted to hear.

Anyway, could this be an excuse for her to keep in contact with the elusive man?

'I promise, Joe, on condition that you let me cook you a meal to say thank you.'

'Thank me for what? You already did more than your share after I had that argument with the bullock. All I've done is promise to listen.' He seemed quite uncomfortable with her suggestion, his cheeks going an endearing shade darker.

'And you took care of me when I fell apart after the wedding,' she reminded him, determined that she wasn't going to let him off the hook even if it meant bringing up that embarrassing loss of control again. 'Now, where's it going to be? Your place or mine?'

The sound of a throat being cleared startled both of them. Joe was the only one who seemed relieved by the interruption. Vicky was cross, especially as she was certain he'd been about to agree.

'Can I help you?' she asked crisply when she turned to face the man standing in the doorway to the office.

For just a second there was something unsettling in his expression as he looked at Joe but then he slid into a pleasant smile as he held out his hand.

'I came to show my face. Grant Naismith, locum,' he said. 'I sent a patient into the hospital last night and thought I'd combine a visit to check up on her with a look around. Actually, I think we might have met before,' he said when he turned to Vicky. 'I believe we trained at the same hospital.'

Vicky conceded that they must have been there at the same time, but silently she couldn't say she remembered him particularly. But, then, she hadn't been interested in anyone else but Nick in those days.

He held Vicky's hand just a little longer than he should have and his pale grey eyes were leaving her in no doubt that he liked what he was seeing. It was a shame she didn't feel the same way about him and just seeing him standing beside Joe was enough to tell her why.

He might be nearly the same height as Joe—about six inches taller than her own five feet six—and his face might be prettier than Joe's rugged taciturnity, but there wasn't the same instinctive attraction towards the man of absolute integrity and hidden strength that she knew Joe to be.

'Which patient did you send in?' She used the pretence of needing to check the screen on the computer to put a little more distance between them. She had to behave in a professional manner towards him even though she was exasperated with him. If he hadn't arrived at that precise moment she was sure she could have persuaded Joe to let them spend the evening together.

'Mrs Frawley.' He mentioned the name of the nearby practice for which he'd been standing in as locum.

'No. We haven't got her here. What was wrong with her?'

'She's an elderly lady and she was in a lot of distress when I saw her. According to her notes she's got a history of heart problems.'

'If she's elderly, she's probably gone to Geriatric,' Vicky pointed out. She was hoping to hurry him on his way before Joe decided to leave without agreeing to her suggestion.

'I tried there first but they said you were taking their overflow at the moment.'

Vicky tapped in another code to cross-check and couldn't find any reference to a Mrs Frawley, until she checked the last option.

'I'm sorry, Dr Naismith, but Mrs Frawley didn't survive the journey to hospital. She's listed as dead on arrival.'

There was a brief flash of emotion in his pale grey eyes before it was swiftly hidden behind lowered lids.

'Not a good start,' she heard him say under his breath, and found herself sympathising. It couldn't be easy, feeling you'd let down a colleague when taking care of his patients. 'Are there any formalities I need to comply with, as I was called out to her, or will the hospital have done the certification? I haven't been in this position before.'

'If you like, I'll take you down to Records and show you how our system works,' Joe offered, and Vicky had to stifle a growl of frustration.

Now she wasn't going to get the chance to speak to him alone, and who knew how long it would be before they had the chance to spend any time together? She certainly wouldn't sink to using this telephone pest as an excuse, no matter what the temptation.

Joe ushered Grant Naismith out into the corridor but at the last second looked back over his shoulder to murmur, 'Seven o'clock at my place, but you'll have to bring the ingredients.'

The couple of hours Vicky spent preparing the meal with Joe and then sharing it in the informality of the warm farmhouse kitchen were everything she could have wished.

They had worked together as seamlessly as though

they'd done the same thing dozens of times before. Even their conversation had felt comfortable, with topics ranging from music to art and books before finally degenerating to the perennial topic of the Denison Memorial.

It's almost as if we're an old married couple, she thought as she began to pile their plates together. Then he passed her a handful of cutlery and when his fingers brushed hers she could have sworn that she heard the crackle of electricity in the air.

The knives and forks fell onto the plate with a noisy clatter and she hastily grabbed them and turned towards the sink to hide her flaming cheeks.

'Sorry about that. I must be getting clumsy in my old age,' she muttered as she plunged them into the hot soapy water.

'You're probably tired. Why not leave the dishes and go home for an early night? Anyway, you did most of the cooking so I should be on clean-up duty.'

'You helped with the preparation, too,' she pointed out as she attacked the remnants of the marinara sauce with a scouring pad. 'Besides, I don't like leaving without finishing the job properly.'

Finally she realised that if she was taking delight in something as mundane as sharing the washing-up with Joe, it was definitely time she was on her way.

Even then, she couldn't stop the little leap of pleasure when he walked her out to her car or the way he watched her driving away. It certainly satisfied that hungry place inside her that wanted nothing more than that he should...

That he should what?

Notice her? See past the end of his nose? Realise that she was the woman he'd been waiting for?

'Right!' she scoffed aloud. 'He's barely done more than wish you a polite good morning in the last six months and suddenly, on the strength of a roadside rescue and a home-cooked meal he's going to take another look at you? Get a life!'

Vicky was still muttering under her breath when she swung her front door open, juggling an armful of uniform brought home for washing and a bag of groceries that had developed a rapidly growing split in one side.

The first thing she saw in the darkness as she reached out for the light switch was the winking red indicator on her answering machine.

It was so rarely used that she was almost excited by the event, dropping her burden just inside the door to press the replay button. Because all her friends knew where she worked, they were far more likely to ring her at the hospital. In fact, very few of them knew her home number as the new directory hadn't been updated since she'd moved into her little cottage and had the phone connected.

The little indicator told her she had two messages, but when the first played through without a word being spoken, a shiver of dread skated up her spine.

She reached out to stop the machine but it had already clicked to the second message and an awful fascination froze her in her tracks as she heard the same voice break the silence of her cosy home.

'Victoria.'

It was the same voice. That same hateful singsong. But this time it was worse. This time it wasn't a call to the hospital where anyone could contact her. This time, whoever it was had discovered her private number and it felt almost as if they'd actually invaded the cottage.

Vicky was still staring at the baleful red eye when the phone rang, the sudden sound startling her into a shriek.

It rang again and for the first time in her life she was actually afraid to answer it. It was almost a relief when the machine switched on to answer it for her, but she cringed when the silence began to stretch out without a word being spoken.

She was convinced that it was her tormentor again but Joe's deep voice broke the fraught silence.

'Vicky, it's Joe. Joe Faraday. I just wanted to make sure you got home safely. Give me a call when—'

'Oh, Joe, thank goodness it's you,' she gasped when she'd managed to grab the handset and put it to her ear. Her hand had been trembling so much she'd nearly dropped the thing.

'Vicky? Are you all right?' The concern was so clear in his voice that it actually helped her to gain a little control.

'There were two messages when I got back...on my answering machine,' she blurted disjointedly.

'Not bad news, I hope. Who was it? Jack? Nick? The hospital?'

'It was *him,* Joe,' she said, the eerie way the man had pronounced her name echoing inside her head.

'Him? You mean the voice on the phone at the hospital? How did he get your home number?'

'Why don't you ask me some questions I *can* answer for a change,' she said as a hint of hysteria crept into her voice. 'I don't *know* how he got it. All I know is that there were two messages. One silent one and the other one...' She shuddered.

'Just your name, again, or something more this time?' he prompted quietly, his voice deep and steady, something to cling to in the midst of her panic.

'Just my name,' she confirmed, 'but why is he doing this, Joe? It was bad enough when he was phoning me at work, but this...'

She drew in a shaky breath as she dragged trembling fingers through her hair. She'd left the blonde length loose to tumble over her shoulders this evening, hoping that Joe would notice. *That* had been a complete waste of time, and now seemed totally irrelevant in the face of what had been happening at home in her absence.

'Joe, what if...' The sudden thought was terrifying. 'What if he knows where I live? Can he find out my address now that he knows my phone number?'

'I honestly don't know, Vicky,' he admitted. 'As for the calls, if it was just a matter of changing your phone number, it would be relatively easy. The fact that he's being a nuisance at work isn't quite so easy, especially as so many calls come through automatic exchanges. If it was the old-fashioned telephone operator we'd have some sort of control.'

The way he'd slipped into saying 'we' instead of 'you' hadn't escaped her. It was strange how much comfort she could draw from something so simple.

'As for knowing where you live...' Joe's voice drew her back to the unpleasant speculation. 'In a place as small as Edenthwaite, he wouldn't have to ask very many people before he found someone who could give him directions.'

'This is one of those times when it's definitely a disadvantage to have been born locally,' she complained. 'All too often I have patients coming in who insist on telling me in great detail about something that happened in my childhood, or even my parents' childhood.'

'That's one of the penalties of being in such a "public" profession. Everyone knows about the local doctors and their families.'

'And they're only too happy to gossip when we get ourselves into mischief,' Vicky agreed.

'They must have had plenty of practice with Jack around, or did he do most of his roistering after he went away to train?'

The conversation continued for several minutes before Vicky caught sight of the time.

'Oh, Joe, I'm sorry. I've kept you up and you've got to be at the surgery early tomorrow.' She couldn't be sorry about the time they'd spent together, even if it had been at opposite ends of the telephone.

'I'm hardly so old and decrepit that I'll fall apart if I miss an hour's sleep,' he objected. 'Anyway, I don't mind. It's worth it to hear you sounding more relaxed. I'll see you tomorrow.'

It sounded almost like a promise and Vicky's heart was feeling immeasurably lighter when she finally put the phone down.

It wasn't that she needed a man in her life to validate it. She had grown strong and self-reliant in the years that she'd pined hopelessly after Nick, concentrating on her career and making her own way in the world.

That didn't mean that she couldn't appreciate the fact that Joe was concerned for her safety. As he'd suggested, she made a point of checking around the cottage to make sure that all bolts and locks were fastened securely.

'Tomorrow, I'll change my number,' she muttered decisively. 'And I'll make some enquiries about the new laws about stalking.'

Part of her didn't want to believe that it was really happening. That same part was trying to tell her that by simply changing her number she would put whoever-it-was off, and she'd never hear from him again.

Unfortunately, the more rational half knew that this was unlikely. The calls had started several days ago and had already escalated from silent calls at the hospital to a verbal one at her home. It might only be one word, just her name, but there was something about the tone of the man's voice that made her feel uneasy.

Remembered scraps from a programme she'd glimpsed on television told her that many stalkers were satisfied just to observe. It was the ones whose observations grew into a need to make contact and from thence into total obsession that had her listening for noises outside her cottage.

It was a good job she'd already eaten her meal. The nervous cramping of her stomach would have left her with little appetite now. The trouble was, with nothing urgent to do and a busy day ahead, the only logical thing was to go to bed.

A leisurely bath was out of the question. She would feel far too vulnerable to relax. Even climbing into bed and pulling the covers right up to her nose didn't make her feel totally safe, no matter that the cottage was securely locked.

It was only when she remembered Joe's final words—a promise that all she needed to do was phone him and he would come to her—that she was able to unwind enough to fall asleep.

CHAPTER THREE

'ANY more phone calls?' Joe asked later on the next afternoon.

The sound of his deep voice set Vicky's heart beating in an erratic rhythm. She had to concentrate to make sense of the words, especially when she was looking up into those gorgeous eyes. They seemed more green than brown today and filled with the concern she usually only saw focused on his patients.

He couldn't have known that she'd just put the kettle on for a much-needed break, but Vicky was delighted with his timing. This way, if she was lucky, she might have a chance to talk to him without interruptions.

'There might have been two,' she said as she poured milk into both mugs and topped them up with tea. 'But I'd had a quiet word with a couple of members of staff at the beginning of my shift. I asked them to offer to take a message from any male callers and to say that I would get back to them.'

'Clever!' he said with an admiring smile. 'So it looks as if you've spiked his guns.'

'I hope so.' She opted to lean back against the edge of the sink rather than join him at the tiny table. As it was, she was all too aware of the scent of the fresh Cumbrian air that clung to his skin and his clothes, even from the other side of the room.

'I also contacted the telephone company this morning,' she went on, determined to keep her mind off the way his dark hair had been tousled by the breeze. He must have walked around the building to reach her department rather than braving the interminable corridors and stairs.

'I explained what's been going on and I didn't even have to ask them to change the number. Apparently, the new anti-stalking guidelines mean they'll organise it as soon as they're notified that there's a problem. I've decided that until the number's been changed I'm going to leave it off the hook when I'm home, and I've switched the answering machine off completely so there won't be any nasty surprises on it.'

'Won't that be a problem for you, not having a message facility? I'm sure there must be a spare mobile you could have in the interim.'

'It shouldn't be necessary. It's not as if I'm on call, like GPs and midwives,' she said dismissively, hoping she was managing to hide how much his concern mattered to her. She really shouldn't let herself believe that it had any relevance—after all, much as she would like it to be, it wasn't any more than his usual concern for his patients.

'Even so,' he said firmly as he leant round her to rinse out his cup, 'I don't like the thought that you might end up stranded somewhere at the mercy of some nutcase. If you call in on your way home, I'll make sure that there's one left for you at the reception desk.'

Joe's proximity must have temporarily disabled her brain because she hadn't even thought of objecting to his bossiness until he'd left the room, and by then it was too late. Anyway, the thought that he was determined to take his concern to practical lengths was oddly pleasant.

'Contrary female. If Jack had tried that on, you'd have shoved women's lib up his nose until he begged for mercy,' she muttered under her breath as she rinsed her own cup and prepared to return to the ward. There were visitors due shortly and she needed to make sure everything was ready for the day's heaviest influx.

At least she had a full complement of staff this shift, even if they were up to a maximum head count on patient numbers. The fact that they still hadn't managed to transfer any of the high-dependency cases back across to Geriatric was something they were just having to make the best of.

Owen, their fifty-eight-year-old Down's syndrome patient with a broken leg, wasn't even waiting until he'd been fitted with a walking cast. He had been causing chaos, seeming to spend most of his time trying to work out how to disconnect all the pulleys to release the traction on his leg.

Vicky had been at her wits' end until she'd realised that the attraction was the television at the other end of the ward.

With all the equipment surrounding his bed, moving him closer to the set wasn't an option. In the end Vicky had contacted Marc Fletcher to ask him to pull some of his hospital manager's strings.

The result had been the appearance of a small portable television complete with a remote control which would probably need to be replaced by the time Owen left.

'Sister, I don't know how we can ever thank you enough,' his carers said when they'd witnessed the transformation in their charge. 'It'll be worth buying him his own television to see him this happy. Mind you, I don't know how his neighbour puts up with having the channels changed every few minutes.'

Vicky had reassured them that it wasn't a problem, but she didn't tell them that the constant changes wouldn't make much difference to Owen's neighbour as he was profoundly deaf and far preferred to read his book.

'Hey, Vicky, how are you doing?' her brother asked, his arrival just in time for a cup of tea unlikely to be an accident.

'I'm fine. And you?' She busied herself with a second mug to stop herself groaning aloud. Ever since her marriage to Nick had been called off, Jack had been turning up at intervals to check up on her. Did he think she was suddenly going to collapse into floods of tears?

The fact that she *had* cried, but all over *Joe's* shoulder, was no one's business but theirs. Anyway, the tears hadn't been about the fact that Nick was marrying someone else. She'd already explained, several times, that the decision to call a halt had been a mutual one. If Jack couldn't accept it, that was his problem.

He was frowning a little as he inspected her face, almost as if he was trying to read her mind, but in the end had to give up the attempt. Vicky could only hope that she'd finally learned not to wear her heart on her sleeve. The whole world seemed to have known about her teenage crush on Nick. She was going to be much more careful in the future.

'Have you heard about this?' Jack asked as he unrolled the brightly coloured flyer he'd brought with him. 'One of the patients, a farmer, brought some copies into the GP surgery today and asked if we could put them up around the hospital.'

'"Easter Barn Dance".,' Vicky read aloud, smiling at the pictures of dancing rabbits and little yellow chicks all sporting cowboy hats and clothing. 'What's that about?'

'It's a fundraiser-cum-social. Everything's been organised locally—food, music, entertainment. It's in aid of the farmers who were particularly badly hit by the foot-and-mouth epidemic last year. Apparently, they've had their compensation from the Government for the slaughter of their animals, but some of the smaller concerns are living from hand to mouth until they can get their farms properly stocked and running again.'

'What's involved in this barn dance, then?' It didn't really matter. Vicky would probably go purely because it was for a good cause but it would be nice to know what to expect.

'According to my patient there'll be a group doing an exhibition of line dancing, which they then undertake to teach the rest of us. The rest of the evening is more like the country dancing we used to have to do in junior school when it was too wet to play outside.'

Vicky checked the date. 'That's this weekend. They're not giving people much chance to get the word around.'

'I think they're seeing this as a bit of a trial run. If it goes well, they'll run several of them. We might even borrow a leaf out of their book later on when it comes to a fundraiser for the hospital.'

While he was speaking Vicky had been checking the duty roster and found that she *was* going to be free that evening. This could be just the thing to show the world that she wasn't sitting at home, moping about Nick's apparent defection.

'Who are you going to be taking?' she asked. 'I presume this is a couples thing.'

'You know me,' he said with a grin. 'I don't like to plan anything too far in advance, especially something like a date. You never know what might have happened to the relationship in the meantime.'

'Relationship?' Vicky hooted. 'I don't think you've ever kept a girlfriend longer than a couple of days and I don't call that a relationship.'

'Are you any better?' he retorted, startling Vicky with the sudden edge to his voice. 'You eat your heart out for a dozen or more years, and when the guy finally asks you to marry him you back out at the last minute.'

There was something in the unexpected sharpness that made her wonder if her Jack-the-lad brother might not have sailed through his life quite as smoothly as she'd always believed. Was there something hidden in his past that had made him wary of even the most elementary level of commitment? Had she been too wrapped up in her own concerns to notice?

'Well, if neither of us has a ready partner, perhaps we should go together,' she suggested, shelving her intriguing thoughts for later.

'Go with my *sister*?' he exclaimed with every appearance of abject horror, and she burst out laughing.

'That's just what you used to say when Mum asked you to take me with you when you were going shopping or to the library.'

'And you used to needle me about being afraid I'd

lose my street cred with my friends,' he added, readily flashing her one of his trade-mark wicked grins so that she was almost fooled into thinking she'd misheard his earlier unguarded response.

'So, are you still worried about it, or are you willing to risk it?' she taunted, far preferring this sort of sparring to his heavy-handed concern for her.

'Tell you what, if you haven't managed to come up with an alternative, I might oblige you, but strictly on the understanding that this is a one-off occurrence and that you have to be wearing all the right gear.'

Vicky was beginning to wonder if the evening was going to be worth the effort, then a little voice inside her head whispered Joe's name. Would it be worth the effort if Joe were her partner? Was it worth asking him?

'OK,' she agreed. 'In the unlikely event that I haven't found an escort, I shall call on you. And I'll expect you to be wearing the right gear, too.'

Once the idea was in her head, she couldn't get it out again.

It wasn't the dancing that attracted her, although the possibility that she might actually get to spend a couple of minutes at a time in Joe's arms as they whirled and stomped around the floor was a bonus. It was actually the fact that she might get to spend a whole evening with Joe if he could be persuaded that the fundraiser was a worthwhile event to attend with her.

That night Vicky thought long and hard about approaching Joe with an invitation.

In the silence of her cosy bedroom she went over all the things she'd learned about him since she'd joined the staff at Denison Memorial. Everyone seemed to have assumed that he'd been married at some stage but no one seemed to know much beyond that. She'd seen for herself that he seemed to have very little interest in a social life but whether that was because he was genuinely the reclusive sort she didn't know.

Could it be something to do with the absence of his wife? Had it been desertion? Divorce? Death? Could it be because he was still in love with her and could see no reason to admit others into his life?

As for what he thought of her, in spite of the fact that her help after his accident meant that she'd spent more time with him than most, she still hadn't a clue.

Her own heart had begun to perform crazy gymnastics whenever he was near but, apart from the time he'd comforted her, he almost seemed to be avoiding any physical contact with her.

She rolled over to lie on her back and stared up at the oddly shaped ceiling that conformed to one end of the cottage roof.

How did she really feel about the man? Was she in any position to know?

It wasn't that long since she'd been planning her wedding to Nick—something that she'd wanted ever since she'd been an infatuated twelve-year-old. Nearly fourteen years down the road Nick had finally proposed just when she'd been about to 'return home' to nurse in Edenthwaite.

Then she'd met GP Joseph Faraday and something had changed.

It hadn't seemed to matter that she'd loved Nick and had been eagerly waiting for their wedding day.

Each time her path had crossed Joe's she'd become more fascinated with the man.

Eventually, she'd realised that the marriage she'd dreamed of for so long would have to be postponed to give her more time to think. Except she hadn't been able to bring herself to tell Nick while the arguments had been raging inside her own head.

For heaven's sake, how could she not be sure that it was what she wanted after fourteen years of loving the man? Nick was everything she'd ever wanted, so much so that she'd barely looked at another man.

But every time she heard Joe's deep voice—with that sexy Scottish burr that had initially brought James Bond actor Sean Connery to mind—her reaction became more intense. She found herself wanting to know more about him, from the simple things, such as his age and address, to the more complex, such as his opinions and aspirations.

Finally, she became convinced that she wasn't being fair to Nick and, full of trepidation, arranged a long-overdue heart to heart.

To discover that her fiancé had fallen madly in love with Frankie Long, a fellow GP, was a shock but, far more than that, it came as a relief.

Now she had to decide whether there was anything in her fledgling feelings for Joe Faraday that could grow into something strong and lasting. Equally, she had to discover whether he could reciprocate those feelings.

Vicky made herself discount his kindness when she'd fallen apart after Nick's and Frankie's wedding. That could have been nothing more than an extension of his skill and empathy as a doctor. Likewise his concern over those worrying phone calls, thankfully a thing of the past since her number had been changed and her staff were taking messages for her on the ward.

On a more personal level, Joe had been grateful for her help after his accident and he actually seemed to have relaxed enough with her during their shared meal to laugh occasionally.

The more she thought about it, the more she decided that the idea of spending a few hours together at something as innocuous as a fundraiser would probably be a very good way of sounding him out. From what she'd learned about him, he would probably jib at the prospect of a crowd but, as far as she was concerned, that would be one of the advantages. If they were surrounded by other people he would be less likely to realise that she had an ulterior motive in her invitation.

'Now all you've got to do is persuade him to go with you,' she muttered as she rolled over onto her side and squashed a handful of pillow comfortably into the curve between her neck and shoulder. 'It's either that or you're going to have to dress up like Annie Oakley and dance with your brother!'

She carefully ignored the possibility that spending an evening with Joe might spell the end to any dreams she might be harbouring. There were some things she wouldn't admit, even to herself. How could she be totally sure that her feelings towards the man weren't connected to the end of her half-a-lifetime's relationship with Nick?

'Dr Faraday?' Vicky called, catching sight of Joe just as he left the spacious reception area at the heart of the new hospital building. 'Joe?'

It wasn't just his lean height and dark hair that had told her who he was but the fluid, ground-eating strides as he made his way towards the GP unit.

'Vicky?' He'd paused at her voice, turning back to wait for her to approach. 'What can I do for you?'

'You can save me from a fate worse than death, or at least twice as embarrassing as mothers showing baby pictures,' she declared dramatically.

Her heart gave a little skip when she was rewarded for her nonsense with one of those rare grins. She wondered if he realised just how much younger they made him look. With a grin like that, she could all too easily picture him as a little boy bent on mischief.

'So, what can I do for you?' he offered, reaching for her elbow to guide her out of the way of a man on his way towards the GP unit.

Vicky smiled absently at the stranger as she stepped aside, vaguely aware as he glared at Joe that his face was familiar. Most of her concentration was on Joe as she tried to will him into amenability.

'Well, you must have heard about the barn dance. The fundraiser?' she added when he frowned as if he didn't know what she was talking about.

'Ah. The poster with the rabbits,' he said with a quirk to one side of his mouth.

'So, you're going to it?' At least she didn't have to explain everything from scratch.

'I'd actually planned to make a donation instead,' he admitted. 'It's not really…' He pulled a face and shrugged slightly uncomfortably. 'I've never been much of a one for dancing.'

'What? No Scottish reels?' she teased lightly, something inside her going all soft and warm when she saw the hint of colour wash over his lean cheeks.

'Not since I was a bairn being dragged along by my mother,' he confessed roughly, his accent deepening by the second. He gestured towards the GP unit and they began to walk in that direction. The fact that she had no trouble keeping pace with him told Vicky that he'd consciously shortened his stride for her.

'Well, in that case you're already streets ahead of me,' she declared, stretching the truth a little. 'I've done little more than disco dancing and a very wooden waltz at a hospital summer ball.'

'So you'll be avoiding this do, too?' He accepted the wire tray stacked high with paperwork that practice receptionist Mara Frost handed him, and continued towards his room.

'Unfortunately, that isn't one of my options,' Vicky explained as she kept pace with him, warmed that he seemed perfectly happy to continue their conversation even though he had so much to do. 'Jack has decided that I've either got to find myself a partner for the evening or I've got to go with him.'

'Would that be so bad?' he asked lightly. 'From what I've seen, you and your brother get on well.'

'That will all be a thing of the past if I have to go to the barn dance with him,' she said darkly as she turned and propped her hips on the edge of the window-sill, giving the meticulously tidy room a brief glance. There was absolutely nothing of a personal nature on show—not a photo, not even a local landscape on the wall.

She dragged her thoughts back to the matter in hand. 'Going with Jack isn't the problem. It's the fact that if I do, he's told me I'm going to have to dress up in all the Wild West fringes and fancy boots like some stage-struck Annie Oakley wannabe.'

As she'd intended, he chuckled, and she pounced.

'Joe, you will save me from a fate worse than death, won't you?' she pleaded. 'If you'll go to the wretched thing with me, at least I can wear something nondescript, like jeans. I love Jack to pieces but we're completely different characters. I *hate* being in the limelight.'

'He certainly isn't shy,' Joe said with wry under-statement, while Vicky held her breath.

He sighed as he slouched onto the corner of his desk and she was almost certain that he was weak-ening.

She gazed up hopefully into eyes that seemed brown today, shot through with rays of gold as they scanned her face. She was almost ready to scream when he finally cleared his throat.

'We wouldn't have to stay long, would we? Just long enough for Jack to let you off the hook?'

Vicky was so thrilled that she could happily have danced an Irish jig and shouted 'Alleluia.' She knew her face must be one big grin.

'It would be just another short stay, just like Nick and Frankie's reception, I promise.'

'In that case, we'd better decide what time I should collect you and then I shall have to get working. If I don't start soon, I shall still be seeing patients this time next week.'

Vicky's feet hardly felt as if they were touching the floor as she floated out of his room and into the reception area. If she didn't hurry, she was going to be late getting back to her own department, but when she would have sped through with little more than an airy wave, Mara beckoned her.

'A call for you, Vicky,' she said, handing her the phone.

'For me?' Instantly, guilt struck. Had something gone wrong up on the ward in her absence? 'Hello? Vicky Lawrence here.'

It took her a couple of seconds to realise that there was that same awful crackling in the background before a horribly familiar voice whispered, 'Victoria,' in her ear.

A shudder of revulsion tightened every nerve in her body and Vicky felt sick. She was sorely tempted to scream something down the phone but held onto her control by the slenderest of threads.

Without uttering a word, she reached out and cut the caller off before gently replacing the receiver in position.

'Problem?' Mara asked.

'Nothing important,' Vicky assured her, retaining enough of her senses to realise that the staff on the GP unit wouldn't have known to take a message for her like her own colleagues would. It wasn't Mara's fault that whoever it was had found another way to pester her, and to say anything would only involve explanations that she didn't have time for.

It wasn't until she'd walked right through the hospital and was approaching her own domain that a frightening thought occurred to her.

How had her tormentor known that she was going to be visiting the GP unit at that particular moment? Even *she* hadn't known for certain that she would be there. Admittedly, she'd gone towards the unit looking for Joe, but it had been at his invitation that she'd accompanied him to his room.

Had someone seen them talking together? Watched

them walking towards the unit and into Joe's room? Was someone spying on her, and if so, why? What did they hope to gain?

Unfortunately, there were far too many questions and too few answers…none of which would help her to do her job.

The staffing level might be almost normal for the number of patients, but the ward was still very busy, especially as a couple of patients had needed to stay longer than expected.

Mrs O'Herlihy was a case in point. She'd spent a small fortune on cosmetic surgery, initially prompted by an unsightly lump on her top lip.

'It just looked like a pale mole,' she'd told Vicky, the latest in a whole stream of staff and visitors who'd had to listen to the interminable tale. 'Well, not really a mole. More like a soft wart, like you see on Hallowe'en witches.'

Unfortunately, the private clinic she'd gone to had failed to diagnose the lump as a basal cell carcinoma. In merely effecting a partial removal for a good cosmetic result, they had allowed the growth to proliferate into the surrounding tissues for several vital extra months.

This time her surgery had been radical enough to remove all traces of the growth, thereby preventing it from spreading still further.

Although it would be at least another day before the dressings finally came off, Vicky knew that, in spite of the surgeon's best efforts, the scarring to the woman's face was definitely not cosmetically pleasing. During dressing changes she'd seen the way the lip was now twisted into a permanent semi-sneer. The livid purple of the scar would fade in time and could always be camouflaged to a certain extent with make-up. It was the damage to the nerves supplying that part of her mouth that would probably horrify their patient most, especially when she was told that they would probably never recover.

All Vicky could do for now was provide a willing ear for the shallow woman's tale of woe and hope she could find a way to point out that at least her condition had finally been diagnosed before it had done too much damage. She knew of another case, a man this time, who had ignored the problem until he'd needed the complete removal of his nose.

Because of her professionalism, none of her patients would guess which of them had her empathy and which her sympathy. Privately, Vicky found it far harder to relate to an idle woman full of self-pity for her marred beauty than to a hard-working farmer afraid that his prosthetic nose would terrify his little grandchildren.

Still, Mrs O'Herlihy felt the need to talk and, although talking wasn't strictly a nursing procedure, Vicky knew that it could have a definite bearing on a patient's rate of recovery.

Being in charge of a television remote control also seemed to be speeding a patient's recovery, if Owen's rate of improvement was anything to go by.

In spite of his carers' dire warnings, none of the staff had experienced a moment's problem with him—at least, not since he'd accepted that he had to surrender the magic gadget when it was time to go to sleep. One episode of a loud late night programme being switched on unexpectedly by a wakeful Owen had been quite enough.

The physiotherapist had even worked out a system

of rewards for work well done, the details of which
had been adopted by the children's ward, too.

'Excuse me, Sister. Could I have a quick word?'
The polite voice interrupted Mrs O'Herlihy's mono-
logue and Vicky was guiltily aware that she'd allowed
her mind to wander.

'That's the trouble with hospitals these days,' the
woman said petulantly when Vicky made her apolo-
gies to attend to her junior's query. 'Everybody's so
busy trying to fulfil some government target that they
haven't got time to speak to the patients any more.'

Her expression was sour when she settled back
against her pillows and Vicky cringed when she con-
templated the moment of truth when the dressings
finally came off. It didn't help to know that all of her
staff tended to steer a wide berth around the woman.
She was just such a complaining sort, with more tales
of woe than...

Enough.

It wasn't like her to let patients get under her skin,
no matter what they did but, in all honesty, it really
would be a relief when the woman went home. Was
that the result of trying to keep her mind off the nuisance caller? He'd certainly been hovering at the back
of her mind like a big black cloud.

In the meantime, Leigh was waiting to speak to her
and there was a mountain of paperwork to climb before the end of her shift.

At least she had the prospect of Joe's company at
the barn dance to look forward to. That should keep
her spirits up.

CHAPTER FOUR

VICKY cursed softly under her breath as she carefully manoeuvred her car out of the corner parking space. It had taken her nearly five minutes—five minutes she couldn't afford—to avoid the thoughtless person who had nearly blocked her in.

The annoying thing was that she was parked in a clearly marked area designated for members of staff, and she had a sneaking suspicion that this one belonged to a visitor. She certainly hadn't recognised the guilty car. If she had, she could have phoned them in the hospital to ask them to move the wretched thing.

When a break came in the traffic she accelerated, barely remembering in time that there was a speed limit on that road.

She fumed as she crawled along on the empty road. If she didn't get moving, she was going to be late. Joe would arrive before she was ready, and she hadn't a clue what she was going to wear and she needed to wash her hair after a day spent working hard in a centrally heated building.

A glance in the rear-view mirror had her exclaiming aloud. A car had just drawn up stupidly close behind her and, if she wasn't mistaken, it looked very much like the one that had blocked her in at the hospital.

Well, there was nothing she could do about it while they were travelling along the road. She would have to be content with thinking evil thoughts about the wretch. Anyway, she didn't have time to confront whoever it was. She had an Easter barn dance to get ready for.

As she pulled into her driveway the other car accelerated past and was gone before she could think about memorising the number. All she could hope was that his brand of thoughtlessness wouldn't endanger any lives.

By the time the doorbell rang it looked as if every item of clothing she possessed was draped over her bed, her chair and the floor.

How could she choose when she didn't really know what mood she was trying to evoke?

One pile was definitely too dressy for a barn dance—far more suitable for a formal ball. Another was too casual and summery for this time of year while another wasn't suitable for the sort of dancing she would be called on to perform tonight.

Finally, she'd donned a pair of dark blue slim-fitting jeans that made her legs look at least a mile long and a shirt-style top that was only a shade or two darker blue than her eyes. The heels on her boots were an indulgence that she might live to regret if the dancing grew too energetic, but she loved what they did to her appearance. Anyway, even with heels on, Joe would be several inches taller than her five feet six. She wouldn't want him to get a crick in his neck if they did get to the stage of having a goodnight kiss.

Her cheeks were still warm as a result of that forbidden thought when she pulled the door open.

'Would you like to come in while I grab a jacket?'

she invited, hoping that her voice didn't sound as breathless to him as it did to her own ears.

As she always saw him at work, she'd only ever seen Joe in suits before. The man stepping into her narrow hallway could have been a different person altogether.

What he did for a pair of jeans ought to be illegal, Vicky thought while she tried to drag her eyes away from him.

His legs looked every bit as long as they did in a suit, but in denims worn just soft enough to outline the body they covered, she could see that his legs had far more muscles than she'd realised. They were long and lean and powerful—an athlete's legs—and when he turned to close the door behind him, she saw that they were perfectly complemented by the sort of backside that made her hands itch to cup it.

For heaven's sake! she chastised herself when he turned and nearly caught her ogling him. Did she really want to spoil the evening before it started?

She needn't have worried about him noticing where her eyes had strayed. He was too busy looking around the little he could see of her home.

'This is almost like a doll's house!' he exclaimed with a smile.

'What else do you expect on a nurse's salary?' she retorted swiftly, her feelings hurt by his scorn. 'But at least it's all mine...well, mine and the bank's until I finish paying for it.'

'Hey, don't get defensive, Vicky.' Joe held his hands up as if she were threatening to shoot him. 'That wasn't what I meant at all. I think it's perfect— so compact. I bet it doesn't take nearly as long to clean as mine, and far less money to heat, too.'

'More than you'd think,' she contradicted darkly. 'There are a couple of windows that need attention as soon as I can afford it.' She paused, but she knew it needed to be said. 'I'm sorry for jumping down your throat, but it's been a bit of a sensitive subject since Nick and I reached the parting of the ways. I over-reacted.'

'Why so sensitive—if you don't mind me asking?'

It wasn't something she'd have discussed with any of her colleagues, but with Joe it felt right.

'Just that some of my shallower colleagues have been pointing out that I should have hung onto Nick while I could. Then I could have been moving into a bigger and better house rather than this little *doll's house*.'

His dark eyes were very intent on her face and she was feeling slightly uncomfortable by the time he finally spoke.

'And do you regret it?' he asked softly, and something in his voice told her that for some unfathomable reason her answer mattered.

'Certainly not for the sake of moving into a bigger and better house,' she said firmly.

'But for other reasons?' he probed with strange insistence.

'The fact that it was the end of a dream is sad,' she admitted with a burst of honesty that surprised her. 'But once I realised that what I felt towards him wasn't enough to sustain a marriage, I knew that I couldn't marry him. At least, this way, we've been able to stay friends. If it had come to a messy divorce…'

His thoughtful nod told her that he'd followed her reasoning and, more, that he'd agreed with it.

'So, now you need to let the world know that you're still alive and firing on all cylinders.'

'Well, at least I need to show my face, and preferably *not* with my brother as my escort.'

'That *might* give people the idea that there aren't any willing escorts around,' he agreed. 'Until you get into the swim, you'll have to call on an old flame or two.'

'No need, while I can call on handsome Dr Faraday,' she said brightly, hooking her hand through his elbow and smiling up at him coquettishly. Not for anything would she admit that there *weren't* any old flames to call on.

The noise greeted them in a hot pulsating wall of sound as they entered the hall.

'Are you sure you want to do this?' Joe mouthed, his words almost completely lost under the barrage of amplified music and competing voices.

'Yes!' she shouted back, grabbing his arm and dragging him into the throng. 'It looks like fun!'

Vicky had never tried it before but she'd seen enough of it on television to know that line dancing was in progress. Her feet were already tapping to the lively beat while she tried to make sense of the instructions sung out by the caller.

'Do you want to join in on this one, or shall we wait till they start again?'

'Let's get a drink first. That looks like thirsty work,' Joe said hurriedly.

Vicky laughed. 'Coward!' she taunted. 'I'm not going to let you escape that easily.'

They met up with several other members of staff at the bar. When the inevitable invitation was made to join them at their table, Vicky found herself holding her breath.

When she heard Joe making the excuse that they were going to be dancing in a minute, she released it in a sudden rush, only realising at that moment just how much she'd wanted to keep him to herself.

She deliberately ignored the speculative looks the two nurses sent their way as Joe ushered her to the other side of the room.

Let them wonder, Vicky thought with more than a hint of smugness. She knew she would probably be in for some quizzing by the time the grapevine got hold of the information, but that wasn't going to be allowed to spoil her time with Joe.

'I'm sorry to have turned their invitation down without asking,' he said into the relative silence of the end of the dance, a frown pinching his brow. 'Are you sure you wouldn't rather sit down at a table?'

'What, and have to talk shop when I could be enjoying your company instead?' she teased. 'No, Joe. Honestly. I'd rather spend the time with you.'

He was silent for a moment before she caught a glimpse of the wicked smile that always put a skip in her pulse.

'It'll help to keep them all guessing, won't it?' he said, just as the caller announced the title of the next dance.

'Especially if I look as if I'm having fun,' she agreed with a hint of a challenge.

He took it up without a second's hesitation.

'You'd better hand that glass over, then,' he ordered, holding one hand out. 'You and I have an appointment with the dance floor.'

The following five minutes had her helpless with

laughter as the two of them tried to follow the moves that everyone else seemed to pick up so easily.

'Are we the only ones who haven't done this before?' he demanded when they turned the wrong way yet again and nearly caused a major calamity. 'Perhaps I'd better get us off the floor before we injure someone.'

'Don't you dare!' she spluttered through a do-si-do in the wrong direction and the inevitable collision with her unfortunate neighbour. 'We'll get the hang of it in a minute.'

Joe muttered something unprintable under his breath and Vicky stifled a giggle, determined to concentrate harder. But it was difficult when she couldn't keep her eyes off the man. She'd never seen him like this, all hot and bothered with his dark hair tousled and his sleeves rolled up to his elbows.

'Watch one of the people in the electric blue satin shirts,' her neighbour said suddenly, pointing to a skinny woman with miles of fringes sewn to her shiny western-cut shirt and a black stetson on her head. 'They're dotted all around the hall so we can follow what they're doing.'

Vicky passed the information on to Joe and within minutes they were both managing to give the impression that they knew what they were doing.

All too soon the music ended.

'At least we finally got the hang of it,' she said as they made their way back to their glasses.

'It should be relatively simple once you know what the caller is talking about,' Joe agreed as he raked his fingers through his hair to restore some sort of order. 'I was beginning to wonder whether I was going to have to admit defeat.'

'You? Admit defeat? Never!' Vicky laughed up at him. 'I don't think the word is in your vocabulary.'

She turned to share the moment with him and was in time to catch a glimpse of a wintry expression in his eyes. She shivered, wondering what had put it there, but this was neither the time nor the place to ask.

'You two seem to be enjoying yourselves,' Jack said, appearing suddenly beside them.

Vicky couldn't help the burst of laughter when she saw how he was dressed.

'Joe, I will be in your debt for ever!' she exclaimed. '*This* is what you saved me from!'

Admittedly, it wasn't shiny blue satin, but there was still an awful lot of fringe on Jack's Davy Crockett suede jacket and as for his hat... It might not hold ten gallons but it certainly looked as if it could manage two.

'I see what you mean,' Joe said with a perfectly straight face which completely belied the humour brimming in his eyes.

'Hey! I resent that!' Jack exclaimed. 'There's nothing wrong with my outfit. It's all genuine western gear.'

'Western Hollywood,' Vicky taunted. 'I doubt that a real cowboy would be caught dead in it.'

'Now, now, children. Party manners,' Joe said, clearly fighting the need to laugh aloud. He took Vicky's hand and she delighted in the chance to thread her fingers between his. 'If you'll excuse us, Jack, we have a date with a dance floor.'

They stayed on the floor after that, giving each new dance a go and finding that it did actually get easier.

Not that Vicky could have cared one way or the

other. With Joe's undivided attention she would have enjoyed herself whatever she was doing, in spite of the fact that she had the uncomfortable feeling that there were eyes watching everything they did.

All too soon it was time to eat and she held her breath, wondering whether this was the moment Joe suggested they'd spent long enough at the dance.

When he suggested that they join in the line for the buffet and then found a relatively quiet corner to sample their selection, her delight almost tempted her to do a thoroughly juvenile handstand.

As it was, she basked in the opportunity to spend time in idle conversation, comparing likes and dislikes in their choices in books and music and bewailing the limited viewing choice at the nearest cinema.

By the time the second part of the evening began she was ready for the change in pace.

This time it wasn't line dancing from America but country dances from England and Scotland, and this time she would have the chance to feel Joe's arms around her.

Some dances she vaguely remembered from her school days. There could be as few as eight people in their set and she had to dance with each of the other men until Joe came round again. Some she vaguely recognised as members of staff or old family friends and one or two tried hard to make conversation in the brief time they had together. One even tried to persuade her to dance with him later, on the grounds that they were old friends.

To be polite Vicky had to make a reply, but her distracted words were probably more than a little dismissive, her interest focused on the tall man courte-

ously partnering another woman when she wanted it
to be *her*.

She knew it was crazy, knew that she shouldn't be
so attracted to the man when she'd had so little time
to get to know him. But she couldn't help the way
her eyes followed him and the extra beat her heart
gave every time he took her hand in his.

But it was when Joe took her in his arms for the
final waltz of the evening that she knew she no longer
had a choice in the matter.

He drew her into his arms, one hand holding hers
against the steady beat of his heart while the other
cradled her head in the curve of his shoulder.

She drew in a steadying breath as the music began
and inhaled a blend of soap and musky skin from the
side of his neck. Something deep inside her seemed
to react to the unique mixture, something that recognised that this was the perfect match, this was the
man who tripped all her internal switches to let her
know that she had finally found her mate.

Helpless to do anything other than respond, she
pressed closer and felt Joe tighten his hold on her in
answer.

Without effort their steps matched in the elegant
dance, rhythmic and so totally in tune with each other
that Vicky felt they could be in a world of their own,
her wooden waltz a thing of the past.

He might have been all at sea with the unfamiliar
line dances but this was something at which he ex-
celled, and for those few minutes she revelled in being part of that mastery.

She barely heard the farewells called after them as
Joe led her out of the hall, still enclosed in the

strangely electric cocoon that had contrived to keep the rest of the world at bay.

In silence he ushered her into his car, joined her and started the engine. There was no reason to speak, she realised as he drove out of Edenthwaite and took the road that led towards both of their homes.

She wasn't surprised when he passed his own house and took the turning to her cottage. It seemed only right that he should escort her to her door, her hand reaching for his as though they had come home like this since for ever.

It was only when she stepped into the tiny porch to unlock her door and realised that he had stayed out on the little path that she began to wonder if she'd read the situation wrong.

'Joe? Aren't you going to come in?' she asked, suddenly feeling as gauche as a teenager...except that most teenagers these days probably had more experience with such situations than she did. 'I could make us a drink.'

It was so long before he answered that she was beginning to wish for the ground to open up and swallow her whole.

She'd been so sure that he'd been feeling the same sense of connection as she had; a sensation that had been growing stronger with each dance, each contact between their hands and bodies. Had she really misread the whole evening so badly?

'Joe?' She halted abruptly when she realised that to say any more would have sounded like begging, and she had too much pride for that.

'Vicky, I'd love to come in for coffee but...' He paused and shook his head as though stuck for words, then suddenly stepped forward to grasp one of her shoulders in each hand.

Before she could draw breath to ask what he was doing he'd bent his head to briefly press his lips to hers.

It was over before she knew it was going to happen, before she had a chance to respond, and she was left staring up at him in the reflected light from the lamp she'd left on in her hallway.

'Joe,' she whispered through tingling lips, knowing that her eyes were wide with surprise.

But he didn't hear her, his long legs already taking him down her path towards his waiting car.

She watched him fold himself behind the wheel and put the key in the ignition and saw him remember at the last minute that he'd forgotten to fasten his seat belt. She watched until the red glow of his taillights had disappeared around the corner and she was left standing shivering in the dark.

'He didn't even look back,' she whispered forlornly, dropping the hand she'd raised ready to wave and feeling foolish. Her fly-away hair, the fine blonde strands carefully pinned and lacquered into position for the evening, finally gave up the battle against the vicious little wind whisking round the corner of the cottage and tumbled down the side of her face like a rat's nest.

Suddenly realising just how stupid she was being, she whirled and hurried inside.

'Standing out there like a lemon,' she muttered, raking blonde strands back behind her ear as she filled the kettle and set it to boil, then changed her mind.

She didn't really want a drink. The offer to make one had just been an excuse to spend a little more time with Joe, preferably without the world and his wife looking on.

He obviously hadn't been interested.

Even his kiss—precious because it had been the first one she'd ever received from him—had probably been nothing more for him than a polite convention at the end of a shared evening. How would she know with her limited social life? She'd wasted far too many years yearning after something that had turned out to be nothing more than a mirage.

Was that what she was doing with Joe?

She burrowed her head into the pillow, the covers pulled right up to her ears, and forced herself to take a hard-eyed look at what was going on in her life.

As far as her profession was concerned, she couldn't have been happier. Edenthwaite had been a wonderful place to grow up and it was a lovely place to work. Denison Memorial was everything that was best in a small hospital, perfectly catering to the needs of the immediate community with strong links to the bigger hospitals and specialists further afield.

Her personal life was another matter entirely.

She'd come home and for several blissful months she'd walked around with Nick's ring on her finger and the perfect wedding to arrange.

Although she'd met Joe when she'd been introduced to the various members of staff, she'd noticed little more than that he was a good-looking man but rather sombre for her taste.

It hadn't been until she'd spent time with him on the ward, when he'd sat beside one of his patients during a long night of misery, that she'd recognised the hidden depths in the man.

Cathy Twomey. She didn't think she'd ever forget

the woman's name, or the ache of sympathy at her circumstances.

She couldn't imagine what it must have been like to have lost her husband to a work-related accident just weeks after they'd learned that they were expecting their first child. Perhaps Cathy had been able to pick up the pieces because she'd had a part of him growing inside her.

Her premature labour at just seven and a half months gestation had been distressing, but nothing could have been as devastating as to learn that the baby had already been dead for several days before the delivery.

In the circumstances, the maternity unit had been the last place she'd needed to be, in spite of the fact that they'd had a single room free. With several babies exercising healthy lungs nearby, it would have been too much to have expected the poor woman to endure, so Vicky had prepared one of the rooms in her domain.

Cathy's parents were elderly and obviously found it difficult to take in the fact that they'd lost the grandchild they'd longed for. They certainly weren't in any state to comfort their stricken daughter.

The in-laws arrived towards the end of labour with armfuls of expensive toys and clothes, and Vicky could remember the uncomfortable suspicion that they were looking towards this child to replace the one they'd lost.

When the news of the stillbirth had been broken to them they'd railed against the unfairness of life and had then left without even visiting Cathy.

It had been Joe who'd sat with Cathy while she'd cried bitter tears, Joe who'd listened while she'd rambled almost incoherently about losing everyone she'd ever loved. It had been Joe who'd managed, some time in those deadly dark hours, to persuade her that life had still been worth living.

And in those same hours, while Vicky had unobtrusively come and gone with tea, sandwiches and medication, she'd realised that there was something very special about Joseph Faraday. Something that had called out to her and had connected deep inside, that had woken emotions which had never been wakened before.

The same was true now, months later, and the fact that her engagement was over had nothing to do with it.

She had fallen in love with Nick the first time her brother had brought him home to visit and had loved him for so many years that it had become almost a habit.

He had been the ideal against whom she'd measured every other man she'd met. It had been one of life's ironies that she'd finally been engaged to her idol when she'd met the only man who could have made her question her years of unswerving loyalty.

And she had questioned them. Unwillingly at first but with a growing realisation that, compared to what she was coming to feel towards Joe, her feelings about Nick were a very pale imitation—little more than an overblown infatuation.

The more she thought about him, the more she realised that she had finally met the man with whom she could happily spend the rest of her life, knowing that things were only going to get better. It was chastening to have to admit that, with Nick, she had been looking forward to their wedding day as the high point of her life. With Joe, if they were ever to marry, the day would merely be the start of an engrossing journey through life together.

If they were ever to marry...

Vicky gave a wry chuckle into the darkness of her cosy room. That was putting the cart before the horse, wasn't it? She didn't even know what the man thought about her and she was already imagining the two of them married. Just because he'd kissed her tonight...well, it had hardly been more than a brush of his lips over hers, she admitted with brutal honesty, and certainly nothing to weave a happily-ever-after fantasy around.

No. She'd tried that route before and she wasn't going to go there again. For years she'd fantasised about marrying Nick and had only come to her senses just in time. How could they have ever been happy once they realised that they had actually settled for second best, a milk-and-water imitation of the real thing?

The real thing. That was what she wanted with Joe, what she was more and more convinced the two of them could have together. All she needed to do was find some way to make him believe it, too, and that was going to take more than an evening at a barn dance and a brief peck on her doorstep.

That brief brush of firm masculine lips over her startled mouth featured heavily in her dreams, but it was the doorstep that featured in her waking moments the next morning.

Vicky wasn't late because she always set her alarm early enough to allow for delays, but today she was certainly cutting things a bit fine.

'You shouldn't have lain in bed after the alarm went off,' she scolded herself as she grabbed her bag and glanced quickly round the kitchen to make sure everything was switched off. There wasn't time to stop to make herself any sandwiches today. She'd splash out on something hot at the hospital and count calories and pennies tomorrow instead. Thank goodness there was a clean uniform waiting for her at work because she didn't want to spend time ironing one now.

Still, it had been hard to leap out of bed when the alarm had woken her and carry on as if nothing had happened, especially when her dream had been so vivid and so very detailed, with Joe gloriously naked in her bed and...

She was still replaying the delicious scenario as she stepped out of the door, and it was only the sudden sound of glass smashing that alerted her to the fact that someone had placed a delivery in her tiny porch.

'What on earth...?' It couldn't be milk bottles. It was some time since the milkman had made deliveries this far out of Edenthwaite.

She looked down at her feet to find them surrounded by a scattered arrangement of deep red roses lying amid the shards of a beautiful glass vase, and her heart gave a silly skip.

The vase was beyond saving but the flowers were beautiful. She could smell their heavy perfume as she bent towards them.

Careful to avoid the wicked edges of the glass, she plucked the little envelope from the cleft of the florist's wand and flicked it open, already certain she knew who had sent them.

They must be from Joe, she realised with a happy smile. Who else could it be?

And to have sent red roses… What did that mean? Had their evening together made him realise that his feelings for her were more than just…

The happy anticipation of her thoughts was destroyed the instant she saw the message.

'Victoria.'

The card carried only that single word but it was enough to send a shiver of dread up her spine.

CHAPTER FIVE

'JOE, he knows where I live,' Vicky said, not caring that her voice was full of panic.

He was the first person she'd thought of when she'd realised the significance of the flowers at her feet.

In spite of their innocent beauty she hadn't bothered picking them up, just stepped gingerly over them as though they were some disgusting bug and hurried to her car.

As soon as she'd parked—as close as possible to the entrance for a feeling of safety—she'd hurried into the hospital to find the nearest phone. Joe had been the first person she'd called and he'd arranged to meet her in her little office on the ward. She took it as a measure of his concern that he'd arrived not ten minutes after she'd spoken to him.

'Calm down, Vicky. How can you be sure? Did you contact the florist?' Joe's was the voice of calm reason in spite of the caring expression on his face.

She could have screamed at the timing of this latest episode. He was hardly going to see her as a rational adult woman if she was openly panicking about something as simple as an anonymous delivery of flowers. Still, it was almost impossible *not* to be anxious with events escalating the way they were. It had been bad enough when it had just been phone calls. At least they had been happening at a distance. This had felt almost face-to-face.

'I phoned the florist as soon as I'd spoken to you.

The flowers were ordered by phone and collected by a young lad just before the shop closed yesterday afternoon.'

'A young lad?' His reaction was the same as hers had been when the florist had told her. The voice she'd been hearing on the phone certainly hadn't been that of a young lad.

'Apparently, he brought an envelope in with cash for payment and took the vase of flowers away,' she explained. 'The shop owner didn't see anyone waiting outside, so couldn't tell who was using him as a messenger.'

'Have you ever had a delivery from them in the past? Could that be how your caller got your address?'

'No deliveries. In fact, no flowers at all since I returned to Edenthwaite. Nick wasn't one for showy gestures like that, and Jack certainly wouldn't waste his time sending flowers to his sister.'

'Roses at this time of year are certainly something of an extravagance, so we must be looking for someone with money to burn,' Joe mused aloud. 'Either that, or someone desperate to impress, in spite of the cost.'

'Not a Scotsman, then,' Vicky teased, and received an affronted glare in return before he returned to his deliberations.

'The fact that the flowers were hand-delivered suggests that whoever it is lives locally.'

'I thought that, too, but I just can't think of anyone who would fit those criteria, certainly not among the staff here, or any friends in the area.' She sighed heavily. 'It's just so frustrating because it must be someone I've come face-to-face with. They were close enough to know when I visited the GP unit, for heaven's sake!'

'You will be careful, won't you, Vicky?' Joe said suddenly, his eyes dark with concern. 'Even if you're certain you know who it is, it would be far safer if you didn't confront them, at least not alone.'

'I wouldn't do that,' she assured him fervently. 'I don't even particularly want to know who it is as long as he leaves me alone. I certainly don't want to get too close to someone who enjoys tormenting people and frightening them.'

He threw a quick glance at his watch, the steel band plain and functional against his wrist.

'Vicky, I ought to go if I don't want my patients to start a riot. Are you sure you're going to be all right?'

'I'll be fine,' she promised. 'I doubt that anyone would be stupid enough to try anything on with so many witnesses.'

'Vicky, I don't want to scare you, but until we can flush him out of the woodwork it would probably be a good idea if you made certain you weren't on your own.'

Joe had taken her hand in his, lean fingers tightening warmly around hers as he stood a little closer. Too close for her brain to work with its usual speed.

'You mean, don't give him a chance to take it any further?' she said with a sinking feeling totally at odds with her reaction to his touch.

'Exactly.' He gave her hand a squeeze. 'If he isn't given an excuse to escalate things, he might find someone else more interesting and leave you alone.'

The pager at his belt gave a sharp bleep and he grimaced when he saw the number on the display.

'That's the unit, wondering where I've disappeared to.'

Vicky didn't want him to go but she knew that was just pure selfishness. They both had work to do with people depending on their skills and she forced herself to loosen her grip on his hand.

'Thank you for coming when I needed you, Joe,' she said quietly. 'It meant a great deal that you were willing.'

'I wouldn't wish this sort of thing on anyone, especially my favourite dancing partner,' he responded swiftly, then offered her a hint of a smile. 'After all, there aren't that many willing to chance the esoteric delights of the Dashing White Sergeant and the Military Two-Step.'

'Not even for charity?' His touch of nonsense sent a feeling of warmth through her.

'Not even for charity,' he said mournfully, then glanced guiltily towards his watch again. 'Look, you will keep in touch, won't you?' he said with a hint of urgency in his voice. 'If he contacts you again— in *any* way—I think we ought to bring the police in.'

'The police?' Vicky tried to swallow but the resurgence of fear meant that her mouth was suddenly too dry. 'Do you really think that's necessary?'

'I didn't mean to scare you,' he apologised, startling her by wrapping a consoling arm around her shoulders. 'But if this goes any further, I really think that would be the best option. There are stalking laws in force these days, so you would be taken seriously.'

His pager went off again but she still had to convince him that she was all right before he would leave.

The chill she felt when he removed his arm from

around her was more than a physical one, and that surprised her. She hadn't expected to feel it as an emotional loss...not yet. She'd expected that it would take far longer into the building of a relationship before it felt as if a part of herself was missing when he left her.

A sound outside her office door brought her back to the present with a rush, and she turned to see a man standing in the doorway.

'Can I help you?' she asked crisply, pinning a smile to her face. It wouldn't do for family members to think that the nursing staff had their mind on personal matters.

For just a second she thought she saw a flash of anger in the man's pale grey eyes but then he smiled and she knew she ought to have recognised that strangely pretty face.

'Grant Naismith, remember?' he said shortly, and she could have groaned.

'Of course it is!' she exclaimed, and beckoned him in. 'I do apologise but we've had such an influx of patients since I saw you last that I haven't got all the relatives straight in my mind.'

She gestured towards the kettle in the corner in a silent invitation and when he nodded went to switch it on as she continued speaking. 'You haven't been contributing to that influx, have you?'

'In what way?'

There was an almost musical quality to his voice and Vicky wondered if it would be worth talking to him about the choir that the hospital tried to form for a Christmas concert each year. That was, if he was still going to be in the area. Life as a locum could take him in almost any direction if he was willing to move about.

'Well, how many of our new patients have you sent in? Perhaps you think we don't have enough to do and want to keep us on our toes,' she said teasingly.

'Well, the job of a GP is certainly a lot more stressful than most hospital personnel know,' he retorted defensively. 'They seem to have the idea that it's something of a soft option and certainly nothing praiseworthy.'

'You certainly wouldn't hear that point of view from me,' she countered, wondering what had happened in his past to make him so prickly about his choice of speciality.

'Because of Dr Faraday?' he challenged with a gesture over his shoulder, and Vicky suddenly wondered just how long Grant had been standing outside her office. Had he overheard her conversation with Joe? Had he seen the comforting arm around her shoulders?

'Not just him,' she corrected coolly. 'My father and my brother are also GPs, so I've always known exactly what the job entails.'

She'd handed him his cup of black coffee and was now wishing she hadn't offered him a drink. There was something about the man's attitude that rubbed her up the wrong way and now she was going to have to wait for him to finish before she could get rid of him.

Still, there were no rules stipulating that she had to socialise with the local GPs. Her best option as far as he was concerned was to stick to being professional.

'So, which patient did you want to check up on today?' she asked, grateful to slip into her Ward Sister persona as she settled herself at her desk. The computer was ready to reveal all sorts of data at the touch of a button.

It was his turn to look uncomfortable, his gaze flitting around the room as though he couldn't bring himself to meet her eyes.

'Actually, this time it wasn't a patient that brought me here,' he admitted. 'I was wondering...well, if you would like to go out...for a drink, perhaps.'

He finally met her eyes, his own pale grey gaze almost too intent.

It wasn't the first time Vicky had wished that it was permissible to say a blunt 'No, thank you'. Unfortunately, polite society demanded that refusals were wrapped up prettily.

'I'm sorry,' she began, trying to dredge up a smile at the same time as she fabricated a believable excuse. When she saw his face settle into an expression of resentment she decided to opt for honesty. 'Look, I hope you don't think I'm being too forthright, but I don't feel I know you well enough to accept your invitation.'

'You'd get to know me if you accepted,' he interrupted bluntly, his tone noticeably less musical.

'Apart from which,' she continued doggedly, ignoring his interruption, 'you're almost bound to have heard from local gossip that my engagement only ended a matter of weeks ago. I'm really not interested in looking for any new involvement.'

Well, it was all true as far as the words went. She *had* ended her engagement to Nick and she *wasn't* looking for a new involvement because she already considered herself involved with Joe. Not that any of that was Grant's business.

His jaundiced expression told her that he hadn't accepted her reasons, and she wondered again just how much he'd seen of her meeting with Joe, but there wasn't really anything he could do about it.

'Well, I reserve the right to ask again some time,' he said smoothly, getting to his feet.

Vicky subdued her sigh of relief until he'd left her office, then she slumped back into her chair.

'What an odd man,' she murmured aloud. He was certainly good-looking enough and apparently had a charming manner with his patients—she'd heard that from several members of staff talking about him since he'd begun working in the area. Female staff, of course, although she couldn't see what they liked so much.

Well, she wouldn't, with her tastes running to tall taciturn Scotsmen with unexpectedly wicked grins.

Perhaps it was just the fact that she had someone stalking her that she was being hyper-alert to strange vibes? The poor man would probably be horrified if he knew she'd lumped him in the same category as the pest who'd delivered the vase of roses this morning.

The memory of the shattered glass she'd left littering her front step that morning was enough to make her groan aloud. She still had that to clear up when she got home at the end of her shift.

In the meantime, she had a ward to run, with junior staff waiting for direction and patients depending on her skills to speed their recovery. Sitting in her office while she pondered the vagaries of sexual attraction wasn't going to get any of that done.

*   *   *

Joe took his glasses off and rubbed both hands over his face, his elbows braced on the top of his desk.

At least there was room for his elbows now. Even a couple of hours ago the whole surface had still been covered with various piles of papers, each coming under a different heading.

He'd been at it for hours, dictating letters to specialists about one patient or another, writing a professional reference for a colleague, replying to an invitation to submit a research paper and another to present a paper at a conference.

Then there had been the pile of forms and information bulletins that would help to keep the practice up to the mark and the never-ending reams of publicity singing the praises of the ever-more-sophisticated remedies being brought out by the multinational drugs conglomerates.

He'd once calculated that it took exactly the same amount of time that he spent face-to-face with his patients as it did to complete the relevant paperwork.

It had taken absolutely hours to catch up with all of it, and there was no reason why he should have decided to tackle the whole lot in one fell swoop like this...except it was the only thing he could reasonably find to do that would legitimately keep him in the hospital while Vicky was still on duty.

'What a thing to choose to do when you had half a day off,' he muttered in disgust. 'And just for a change the sun was shining, too.'

It would have been wonderful to have put his walking boots on and made for the fells surrounding his farmhouse. He could have been out in the open, surrounded by clean fresh air and the lyrical drifts of curlew song, but had chosen instead to closet himself with a mountain of papers.

He couldn't really explain it, but he'd had a feeling that Vicky might need to have him somewhere close at hand. He wasn't certain why, or where the feeling had come from. He wasn't prone to flights of fantasy and had never been interested in anything mystical, but when all the hairs had gone up on the back of his neck he'd known that he wasn't going to go far away.

Vicky hadn't wanted to involve the police, hoping that whoever was targeting her like this would eventually give up and go away. After the latest episode with the vase of flowers, he had his doubts.

The fact that they had been delivered by hand was a definite escalation in the level of threat.

He'd been sorely tempted to contact the police in spite of her misgivings but had settled for spending the rest of the day at Denison Memorial. When it was time for the end of her shift, he'd decided that he'd 'accidentally' bump into her when she went out to her car. Then it would be easy to follow her home and make sure she arrived safely. He'd never forgive himself if something happened to her at the hands of some sociopath when he could have been there to prevent it.

Not that he knew why he was appointing himself as her protector. God knew, he wasn't anyone's idea of a knight in shining armour. He hadn't even been able to save—

He cut that thought off before it could go any further. That was ancient history and had absolutely no bearing on what was happening now. Vicky was absolutely nothing like Celia. She wouldn't take chances with her life.

The trouble was, he wasn't certain that she was thinking clearly these days. She would probably accuse him of patronising her if he were to say anything, but it was a fact that she'd been in love with Nick Johnson for years. No one could switch off that sort of devotion just because the man had fallen in love with someone else.

He'd seen her tears, for heaven's sake! She'd managed to present a brave face to the world but he'd been the one comforting her when she'd broken down after the reception. Then to have this pervert stalking her...

Anger had him clenching his fists and he looked down at them in surprise. It had been a long time since he'd let anything touch him underneath the layer of permafrost he'd cultivated around his feelings.

What was it about Vicky Lawrence that affected him like this? Why did he care what happened to her?

It was hardly a surprise that he would want to see that she was safe. No normal human being could have wanted anything else. But why did *he* want to find a way to ease her unhappiness?

It wasn't as if they had anything in common, apart from their careers in medicine. She was young and beautiful and, in spite of her recent romantic disappointment, she would find someone equally fitting to marry and father her children.

He'd already had his chance at happiness, and with his fortieth birthday looming on the not-too-distant horizon, he knew that the solitary life he'd fashioned for himself was probably as good as it was going to get.

No, if he was honest, he would have to admit that it wasn't completely satisfying and, no, he wasn't really happy. On the other hand, it was better than the alternative. There was no way that he was going to risk putting himself through the soul-searing agony he'd suffered when he'd lost everything that had mattered in his life.

He pressed his fingertips against his burning eyes but still the blonde-haired, blue-eyed perfection that was Vicky Lawrence continued to plague him.

What was it about the woman that he couldn't get her image out of his mind?

It had been bad enough when that image had been of the miserable creature sobbing as if her heart were broken. He could tell himself that it was pity that brought her to mind.

The same wasn't true of the laughing sprite he'd encountered on the dance floor at the barn dance. *She* was totally full of life, her eyes sparkling with infectious good humour in spite of the fact that she was making a mess of the dance.

And when she'd stepped into his arms for that fateful last waltz… He drew in a shuddering breath at the memory.

How could he try to kid himself that she was little more than a child when he'd held the woman in his arms? She'd been tall enough to meet his gaze, tall enough to rest her head on his shoulder, while her body had matched his so tantalisingly at every point.

He could still smell the spring-like fragrance that had surrounded him. He'd ached to find out whether it came from her skin or her hair but had retained just enough self-control to resist the temptation.

He hadn't been able to resist the greater temptation when he'd seen her to her door. She'd turned towards him with an invitation into her cottage and he'd been on the verge of accepting when the sight of her softly parted lips had lured him to succumb to their silent lure.

It had been the briefest brush of his lips over hers and had been over almost before it had begun, but it had rocked him to the core.

He'd thought he'd locked the memories away but she made him remember a past that was best forgotten; the memories of all he'd had and all he'd lost that left him aching with loneliness.

In spite of that, all he could think about was repeating the kiss, only the next time he was afraid he wouldn't be able to stop himself from lingering a little longer. He knew there were all sorts of reasons why he should stay away from her, not least the fact that he was so much older than she was. He was thirty-seven, for heaven's sake, and she was probably twenty-two...twenty-three at the most, with her whole life ahead of her.

Still, something inside him needed to find out whether that strange spark of electricity he'd thought he'd felt between them had just been a figment of his imagination.

Perhaps, if he found out that her kiss was no different than any other, he might be able to put it out of his mind long enough to go to sleep.

'Joe! I didn't think you had a surgery this afternoon,' Vicky exclaimed when she caught sight of him, her heart lifting when she recognised him.

She was on her way out of the hospital, making for the car park at the end of a very long day, and she hadn't expected to see him. From the look of him, he hadn't been home since his surgery had ended, still being dressed in one of the conservative dark suits and pale shirts that he usually wore to work. About the only concession he'd made to the end of a long day was the fact that he'd loosened his tie a little and undone his top button.

'I've been clearing a mountain of paperwork,' he explained, pushing the door open for her with old-fashioned gallantry before following her out. 'If I don't have a real good go at it sometimes, it seems to breed.'

'I know what you mean,' she agreed with feeling, her pace matching his perfectly only because he wasn't striding out in his usual way. 'I thought computers were supposed to be speeding us towards a paperless future, but at the moment it just seems to mean that we have to duplicate everything. It can take hours to track things down, only to find that someone's put a printed copy in one of the piles on my desk.'

It was a perfectly ordinary conversation between two colleagues but somehow it felt so right to be having it with Joe, as if this were something they did every day. She was just wondering whether she dared to ask him to join her for supper when she caught sight of the front of her car and stopped with a gasp.

'Oh, no!' she wailed when she saw the flat tyre. 'That was brand new only a few weeks ago. I must have picked up a nail or something.'

'Only if you picked up four at the same time,' Joe pointed out grimly.

Vicky couldn't believe her eyes. All four tyres were completely flat.

'It looks as if someone used a knife of some sort.

Look.' He pointed to the slash in the wall of the nearest tyre then gestured to the other one on that side.

'Who would have done such a thing?' she demanded in disgust. 'It's such mindless vandalism.'

'I don't think this *was* just random vandalism,' Joe said quietly, and she suddenly felt sick.

'You think it's him, don't you?' she said, feeling sick.

'Especially with this evidence.' He pointed to the surface of the driver's door and she saw what he meant.

Gouged deeply into the paintwork, completely ruining the silver-grey surface beyond repair, was the word BITCH.

'On second thoughts, I think I preferred it when he called me Victoria,' she said with an attempt at humour, then spoiled it with a little hiccup that was more of a sob than a laugh.

'I hate to say it, but this looks like revenge,' he said thoughtfully.

'Revenge for what?' she demanded heatedly. 'I don't even know who he is, so how can I have done something to warrant this?'

'What about the flowers?' he reminded her. 'Perhaps he went past your cottage again today. If he saw the remains still on the step, this could be the result.'

'Well, they were beautiful flowers and I've got nothing against roses, but even if I hadn't knocked them over, there was no way I was taking them into my home,' she said firmly. 'I was so shocked to realise they were from him that I didn't even want to stay there long enough to get rid of them in case he was spying on me from somewhere nearby.'

'That's the trouble with not knowing who he is. It

could be anybody…at least, anybody sick enough to make nuisance calls and vandalise a car just because his flowers weren't welcome. Anyway, it's obvious this isn't going anywhere tonight,' Joe announced with a tap on the roof of the vehicle. 'Grab your things and I'll give you a lift home. We can call the garage out to collect it in the morning.'

Vicky couldn't summon up enough energy to argue, not when she really wanted the comfort and security of Joe's presence close to her.

It wasn't till she looked down at her feet that she realised she'd dropped her bag on the ground at some stage, spilling the contents all over the place.

Suddenly everything seemed too much to cope with and she just stood there staring down at the mess, unable to work out what she was supposed to do about it.

'Here,' Joe said, holding out his keyring. 'Press the right-hand button to unlock the doors and climb in.' He took her by the shoulders and turned her to face the quietly luxurious if slightly mud-splattered car and gave her a gentle push.

Like a zombie Vicky plodded across to settle herself in the cushioned comfort of the passenger seat, only remembering her scattered belongings when Joe climbed in the driver's side and handed her the refilled bag.

'You didn't have to—'

'Shh, Vicky. It only took a moment and it's done now. Just relax,' he said soothingly as he started the engine and turned on the CD player.

She subsided gratefully, switching her brain to neutral and letting the gentle sounds wash over her as he drove her away from the hospital and the forlorn sight of her car.

'Wait here a minute,' he said when he pulled up outside her little cottage, and she didn't even bother to open her eyes, concentrating on the soothing symphony to keep her mind off the chaos that seemed to be starting to surround her.

It wasn't till she heard the familiar sound of her dustbin lid being lifted that curiosity got the better of her and she peered around to see where Joe had got to.

The sight of a handful of mangled roses being summarily dumped in the dark interior of her bin had the tension returning with a crash.

She sighed wearily and released her seat belt. It was time to get back to reality, and that involved clearing up messes rather than sitting listening to music.

'You didn't have to do that,' she said as she climbed out of the car.

'Better to do it now than chance treading it inside,' he said matter-of-factly. Vicky hadn't realised that he must have appropriated her keys when he'd picked up her belongings in the car park until he pushed the front door open for her to precede him. 'I put the kettle on when I went in for the dustpan.'

Surprised, she stopped in her tracks and turned to face him, her eyes almost on the same level with his while he was standing out on the step below her. They were such fascinating eyes, too, their colour seeming to change with his moods. At the moment they were a soft hazel colour and filled with concern for her.

'Joe, has anyone told you lately that you're a very nice man?' she asked. She knew that he couldn't fail

to hear the suspicious quiver in her voice but right at
that moment she couldn't have cared less. 'How did
you know that I was dreading coming back to that…'
she gestured towards the step where the shattered vase
and its contents had lain all day '…and that what I
really need is a large hot cup of tea?'

'Probably because those wretched flowers have
been on my mind, too, ever since you told me about
them,' he admitted quietly. 'And the first thing I *always* want as soon as I get home is a cup of tea.'

There was the sound of a furiously boiling kettle
in the background and they both smiled.

'Well, what are we waiting for?' she asked, and led
the way inside.

CHAPTER SIX

VICKY was in the middle of trying to persuade Joe that it would be no extra bother to cook for two when his pager went off.

'Damn. I've left my mobile in the car,' he muttered as he stood up from his side of the tiny kitchen table. 'I wonder how long they've been trying to contact me.'

'It's a good job my cottage is still in range of the hospital's pager system, then. Use my phone,' Vicky invited, pointing to the instrument on the wall beside the door. She hadn't even realised that he was on call this evening.

There was no point in leaving the room to give him any privacy because the cottage was so small that she'd be able to hear his voice wherever she went. Anyway, she was interested in everything that went on in Joe's life, so she sat back in her chair to eavesdrop shamelessly.

'Dr Faraday,' he said when his call was answered. 'You paged me?'

Vicky knew from the sudden fierce frown that there was something serious amiss, but from his terse questions couldn't tell exactly what.

'I've got to go,' he announced without preamble as soon as he ended the call, his tone grim. 'There's been an accident—a pregnant woman with three children in the car. She's bleeding and the midwife thinks the placenta might have partially abrupted. It was positioned very low in the uterus anyway, so we were going to have to watch it when she went into labour. But that's still some time away.'

The details were beginning to sound ominously familiar to Vicky. 'Joe, it's not Francine Laycock, is it...I mean Francine Latimer. I used to go to school with her. She's one of my oldest friends in Edenthwaite. Oh, God, Joe, she's only twenty-eight weeks pregnant.'

'I'm sorry,' he said as he reached for his jacket, already sliding his arms into the sleeves as he set off towards her front door. 'I've got to go.'

'Wait a second. I'm coming with you,' she called, grabbing her own jacket and her keys and scurrying after him. 'You might need someone to take care of the children. Andy—her husband—is away at the moment and her mother wouldn't be able to get here for hours.'

The hurried journey back to Denison Memorial was fraught with silent tension, both of them wrapped up in their own thoughts.

Vicky had all but forgotten that Joe's speciality before he'd become a GP had been obstetrics and gynaecology. If it was impossible to get Francine to one of the bigger hospitals, he was the obvious person to call in such a situation.

Vicky found herself offering up a prayer for her friend, one of the happiest people she'd ever known and a wonderful mother. She certainly didn't deserve this to happen.

'Just how serious is a partial abruption?' she demanded as the hospital came into sight. 'I mean, I remember what it is from my training—the placenta starting to peel itself away from the wall of the uterus—but what will it mean for Francine and the baby?'

'I won't know until I've examined her,' he said guardedly. 'It sometimes happens spontaneously in a perfectly normal pregnancy. In Francine's case, there could be the added complication of trauma from the accident. If only a small portion of the placenta has come away and there's only a small amount of blood loss, bedrest may be enough to lessen the bleeding and keep mother and baby safe.'

'And if the bleeding doesn't lessen?' She crossed superstitious fingers that they were talking about something purely academic.

'If bleeding continues or worsens, there are complications for both of them. The baby would be starved of oxygen and nutrients and could even die. The mother would be looking at serious blood loss, widespread clotting inside the blood vessels, kidney failure, even death. In that situation, an early delivery would be better for both of them.'

'But it's only twenty-eight weeks!' she exclaimed in horror. 'The statistics on normal survival—'

'I know, Vicky,' he interrupted roughly as he drew up near the entrance of the accident and emergency department. 'Believe me, I know.'

She scrambled out of her side of the car, slamming the door quickly and racing after him.

The sound of children wailing met them as they entered the department. Much as Vicky would have liked to have found out as quickly as possible what the matter was with her friend, she would probably be the only familiar face in a terrifying world. There was clearly some soothing and comforting to be done.

'Hey, Luke! Jake! Fancy seeing you here,' she

called brightly as she hurried towards the five-year-old twins huddled together in a cubicle and sobbing. Their little brother was too young to understand what was happening to his safe little world but he'd obviously picked up on his brothers' misery and was howling inconsolably. The young nurse detailed to supervise the three of them looked well out of her depth.

'Aunty Vicky! Oh, Aunty Vicky,' the twins chorused, and scrambled down off the bed to fling their arms around her and sob against her neck.

Vicky's arms tightened convulsively around them, hoping she would be able to find the right words to answer any questions they threw at her. She'd seen them fairly often since she'd moved back to Edenthwaite to work at Denison Memorial but had no confidence that she would automatically know the right thing to do. Even at five they were too bright to tolerate being fobbed off.

'Aunty Vicky, Mummy had blood on her head,' Luke wailed, or was it Jake? It didn't seem to matter how many times Francine had pointed out the differences between the two boys, she still couldn't guarantee to tell them apart.

'Aunty Vicky, they took Mummy away, and they wouldn't let us go with her,' sobbed Jake, or was it Luke?

At just over a year, Paul wasn't old enough to hold a conversation yet, so he was communicating his distress in the only way he knew how, and doing it at full volume.

'Shush, sweetheart,' Vicky soothed as she released him from his safety seat and tried to cuddle his rigidly disapproving little body. 'I take it they've been checked over since the crash?' she asked the young nurse in an aside.

'Yes. By the paramedic in the ambulance and again as soon as they got here. They were all safely belted in, so they'd come to no harm. It's just their mum…'

Vicky could sympathise with the suspicious gleam that came to the nurse's eyes, but she couldn't afford to let her own feelings show. She had three frightened children on her hands and if Francine could hear their distress, it wouldn't be doing her peace of mind any good.

'In that case, would you like to let someone know that I'm taking all three of them to find something to drink? I expect they're hungry, too.' She knew it was unusual for the children to be out so late. Francine liked to keep to their comfortable routine, especially when Andy was away working. What had happened to put them on that road at that time?

'Do you want me to come with you?' the junior nurse offered, half-heartedly enough that Vicky had to stifle a smile.

'No need,' she reassured her. 'Me and my gang will be all right, won't we, boys? We're going exploring to see if we can find some milk or some orange juice. Which would you prefer?'

The prospect of going exploring for something to drink was enough to distract Luke and Jake and, in the reassuring comfort of her arms, little Paul had subsided to the occasional grizzle and sniff.

As they entered the canteen the twins announced that they were starving and Vicky had a hectic half-hour cutting up sausages for oversized forks and spooning baked beans and scrambled eggs into willing mouths.

With a full bottle of milk and two lidded cups all purloined from other departments in the hospital, Vicky eventually returned to the accident department.

The first person she saw was Joe, but he looked very different from when she'd seen him last.

Gone were the dark suit and smart shirt and tie. Instead, he was wearing a set of green scrubs and looking as if he'd like to pull his hair out by the roots.

'Joe?' She could hardly speak for the lump lodged in her throat. 'What's happened? Is Francine…?'

'No,' he reassured her swiftly, obviously reading her fear from her expression. 'No, Vicky, but she's got a hard decision to make.'

He didn't say any more in front of the children, but he didn't need to. After their conversation in the car on the way to the hospital, Vicky could guess what the diagnosis must have been and her heart ached for her friend.

It also ached for Joe. It must be terrible to have to break such news to a patient. She could tell from the pain she could see in his eyes that this was devastating to him.

He rubbed one hand over his face and the gesture spoke of a bone-deep weariness.

'Aunty Vicky?' There was a tug at her sleeve. 'Where's my mummy? Is she all better yet?'

She looked up from trusting blue eyes into tormented hazel.

'Can I take them through to see her?'

He hesitated for a second then his expression hardened visibly and Vicky shivered at the unexpected change. When he spoke she realised that this was another side of him that she hadn't seen before.

'That might be a good idea,' he agreed. 'Perhaps

you can persuade her that they don't deserve to be orphaned over a principle.'

'What?' she breathed in shock, hardly believing what she'd heard. 'Is it that…?' She'd been about to ask about the severity of the situation but she could hardly do that with Luke and Jake looking and listening and taking everything in, albeit with a child's level of comprehension.

With his glance in their direction she knew that Joe clearly understood her dilemma.

'The ultrasound wasn't good. She won't listen, but we need to do a Caesarean. Now.'

Those few words, carefully chosen to be as incomprehensible as possible to little ears, were enough to paint a graphic picture in her mind.

Vicky quailed at the thought of the devastation it would cause to this precious family if they were to lose Francine. For years now, Andy, Francine and their boys had been in her mind as the Ideal—the perfect family unit she'd wanted for herself if Nick had ever come to love her as much as she'd loved him.

Even with the end of her engagement she hadn't given up on the hope that she would someday achieve her goal.

How much worse would it be if she'd had it all and then lost it?

Mute with misery, she led her bewildered little charges into the room where their mother lay.

Vicky's first sight of her friend was shocking enough to someone who saw sick people on a daily basis. To someone who had known her since they'd been at junior school together, and even more to her tiny sons, it was like something out of a nightmare.

Surrounded by all the noisy paraphernalia of high-technology medicine, Francine was nearly as pale as the white cotton sheet she lay on, her skin looking almost waxy and semi-transparent under the unforgiving lights.

'Mummy?' quavered a worried voice.

To Vicky's relief, Francine opened her eyes, but she could see just how much effort it took.

'Hello, darlings,' she murmured weakly. 'You found Aunty Vicky.'

'She found us,' one of the boys contradicted brightly. 'She gave us sausages and beans. Paul had scribbled eggs.'

'And we had drinks with *straws*!' his twin added, not to be left out. 'Mummy, we don't like it here. Can we go home now?'

The plaintive question was enough to bring the sting of tears to Vicky's eyes. It took real concentration to fight them, especially when she saw Francine losing the battle.

'I know where there's a television that plays videos,' Joe announced into the loaded silence, co-incidentally hitting on the twins' greatest weakness after chocolate biscuits.

'Cartoons?' the twins demanded simultaneously, distracted by the promise of such a treat. 'Can we watch, Mummy?' The request was almost an after-thought. They didn't even notice that their mother was almost too weak to answer, already reaching trustingly for Joe's hands.

He glanced at the child still cradled in Vicky's arms and raised an eyebrow.

'He's nearly asleep,' she murmured, knowing from previous cuddling sessions what that heavy head on

her shoulder meant. 'Leave him with me. You'll have
enough on your hands with Luke and Jake. I'll stay
with Francine.'

The pointed expression in his eyes told her he was
hoping she would do more than just stay with her,
and a longer look at her friend was enough to make
her afraid that they might not have much time to work
with even if she did change her mind.

'Francine?' she said softly, pitching her voice just
above the level of the various sounds of the monitoring equipment. There were various members of staff
moving around them but they were unimportant. At
this moment it was her friend's life that mattered.

'Don't, Vicky,' Francine murmured, sounding utterly weary. 'There's no point trying. I can't murder
my child. It wouldn't be right.'

In the face of such implacability Vicky almost felt
defeated before she'd started. Then Paul stirred
against her shoulder and she was suddenly flooded
with a fierce wave of protective anger.

'I've always known that you agree with your relig-
ion on the abortion debate but I wasn't aware that it
had started allowing suicide,' she snapped, and heard
a concerted gasp from their silent audience.

It brought Francine's eyes open with a jerk, too.

'Vicky!' she protested feebly, and Vicky had to
harden her heart to continue.

'Well, that's what you're doing, isn't it? In fact,
it's murder *and* suicide, now that I think about it,' she
corrected herself. 'You *know* that you're bleeding to
death while you're lying there, and you won't let Joe
do anything about it. That means you're sentencing
your baby to death as surely as if…' She hunted for

the most horrific comparison she could find. 'Francine, it's as if you're cutting its throat yourself.'

'No! That's not true,' she whimpered, trying to find the strength to argue her case. 'The bleeding might stop. Anyway, it's too early. The baby will die.'

'It's going to die anyway if you don't let Joe help you, because the bleeding *isn't* going to stop. Francine, Joe wouldn't be wanting to operate if it were. Anyway, what about the boys? What about Andy?' she demanded, changing tack suddenly. 'Don't you care what happens to *them*? Don't you love them any more?'

'Of course I do,' Francine choked, tears now streaming down her ashen cheeks. 'I love them all, but I love...I love this baby, too.' She cradled the frighteningly small bump at her waist with trembling hands. 'Don't ask me to kill it.'

'I'm *not* asking you to kill it,' Vicky said, almost at the end of her rope. She'd never had to do anything so difficult as to pretend to her dying friend that she didn't respect her principles. '*You're* the one who'll be killing it unless you give Joe a chance.'

She stepped forward and deliberately put her hand beside her friend's. There was no sign of movement. Was it already too late? She wouldn't allow herself to think so.

'Already this baby is running out of oxygen,' she pointed out persuasively. 'How long will it be before he or she is brain damaged beyond rescuing? How long before your own brain starts to suffer, before your kidneys stop functioning? If Joe operates you'll *both* have a chance of living. If he doesn't...'

She had to drag in a quivering breath before she could continue, knowing this was the end of the line.

Subconsciously, she was drawing strength from the solid little body cradled in her arms, knowing she was fighting for his future, too. She took her hand away from the unborn child to stroke the silky head tucked so trustingly in the curve of her shoulder.

'Francine, if you won't let Joe operate, what do you want me to tell Andy and the boys? Have you got any last messages for them?'

There was such despair in Francine's eyes that Vicky could hardly bear to look at them, but she didn't dare to look away.

In the end, it was her friend who glanced away, looking over Vicky's shoulder at something or someone behind her.

'Please, Joe,' she whispered brokenly. 'Please, try to save my baby.'

Until that moment, Vicky had been concentrating so hard that she hadn't realised that Joe was even in the room with them, let alone standing right behind her. Sheer relief that her friend had changed her mind sent her reeling and it was Joe's strong hands that briefly steadied her, one on either shoulder.

'I'll do my best, Francine. I promise,' he said, and with one last squeeze of Vicky's shoulders he was on the move, issuing a stream of orders that the other staff were only too pleased to follow with alacrity.

As hastily as she could on legs that felt like overcooked spaghetti, Vicky got out of the way. Her arms were aching so dreadfully now, with supporting the weight of the sleeping child, that she was amazed that she hadn't noticed it sooner.

She waited until Francine was whisked off towards the west wing, knowing that the minor surgeries unit would have been readied as much as possible to cope with this unexpected disaster.

Then there was nothing more that she could do for her friend other than sit with her children and pray that Joe would be in time to save both lives.

'Vicky,' a deep voice whispered in her ear, drawing her up from the depths of a troubled dream. 'Vicky, wake up.'

She opened her eyes and blinked in the half-light, wondering what on earth was going on.

'Joe?' she murmured in sleepy confusion.

There was only one man with those fascinating changeable eyes, but what was he doing in her bedroom? No, it wasn't her bedroom or she wouldn't be in a chair, twisted up like a pretzel.

'Are you awake?' he whispered with just a trace of that sexy Scots accent in his husky voice. 'Can you come out?'

'Out?' What was he talking about? Come out? It was the middle of the night.

'I don't want to risk waking the children,' he murmured softly.

Remembrance came like a bullet from a gun, eradicating the remnants of sleep. In a flash she knew where she was and why.

'Francine?' she whispered frantically. 'Is she—?'

He halted her question with a hastily positioned finger over her lips.

'Out,' he repeated with a gesture towards her sleeping companions.

The twins had been perfectly happy to share the bed in the single room, after their initial objections to the 'babyish' safety rails. Vicky had finally had to point out that it was a long way to fall onto a hard floor before they'd settle.

Little Paul hadn't been a problem. The portable cot fitted easily into the corner of the room and with a clean nappy, a warm bottle and plenty of cuddles, the youngest of the trio seemed to have accepted Vicky as a substitute mother without a qualm.

All Vicky had been praying for had been that her services wouldn't be needed for very long before Francine was able to take over again. She wouldn't let herself think about any other possibility.

She could have sworn that every muscle in her back creaked when she tried to straighten up, but then she hadn't intended falling asleep, especially not in a wooden-armed easy chair. Desperate to hear the news, she tried to hurry but one foot had gone to sleep and refused to go back into her shoe.

'Stupid things,' she hissed, and kicked both of them back under the chair to hobble out in Joe's wake in her stockinged feet.

'Joe.' She grabbed his arm when he would have led her towards the nearby lounge. 'Please. Just tell me.'

'She's alive,' he said succinctly, but she could tell from his expression that it had been a close-run thing.

'Thank God,' she breathed fervently, then added, 'Thank *you*, Joe. And the baby?' She was almost begging for it to be good news as she looked up into his weary face, even though she knew how unlikely it was.

In spite of her earlier pretence of hard-heartedness, she knew how devastated Francine would be to lose the baby. It didn't matter that she already had three healthy boys. Each baby was equally precious to her.

'She's alive, too, but only just.'

'*She*? She's alive?' Vicky squeaked. Two shocks at once, both of them so wonderful that she could hardly believe what she was hearing. Francine hadn't wanted to be told the sex of her baby. She'd wanted a few months of pretending that it was going to be the daughter she longed for, in spite of the fact that there hadn't been a girl born into Andy's family for five generations.

And in spite of the odds, she was alive!

'What are her chances?' she demanded, knowing she was asking for impossible predictions and hardly daring to hope.

'It's difficult to say until we know how much damage was done by oxygen starvation,' Joe said cautiously. 'On the plus side, there might have been a mix-up with Francine's dates. The baby definitely seems more advanced than the twenty-eight weeks we were expecting.'

'Thank God for that,' Vicky breathed. 'Francine never has had a regular system, right from when she was a teenager. Each one of her due dates has been a bit of a guesstimate.'

'Added to that is the fact that girl babies are usually more fully developed by the time they're full term, so that might be giving us an extra few days of leeway, too.'

'Can I see her? Can I see *both* of them?' Relief and elation were making her quite light-headed. She was very tempted to fling her arms around the man to show him how much she appreciated what he'd achieved tonight.

'You'll have to be quick,' he said, thankfully totally oblivious to her thoughts as he set off at a fast clip towards the ambulance bay. 'Baby Latimer is about to be transferred to the specialist neonatal unit. Having survived delivery, I want her to get every possible chance.'

'And Francine?' Vicky didn't care about professional decorum. After a quick word with Night Sister to keep an ear open for the children, she was openly jogging to keep up with Joe's long-legged stride, her stockinged feet almost soundless on the slick hospital floor.

'When I saw her she was still too groggy from the anaesthetic to make much sense, no matter what I said.'

The night air was chilly as it whistled in through the open door to the ambulance bay, summer still a rather distant dream in Cumbria, but Francine's precious daughter was perfectly safe and snug in her temperature-controlled isolette. Completely self-contained with every sort of monitoring device such a tiny baby could need, it would be her substitute womb until she reached one of the foremost specialist units in the country.

'She's so tiny…so *minute*,' Vicky murmured as the tears she'd been suppressing for so long welled up uncontrollably to spill down her cheeks. 'How can anything that fragile ever have a hope of surviving? Her skin's almost transparent.'

'If she's anything like her mother, she'll be stubborn,' Joe pointed out wryly as the doors closed, shutting the tiny passenger away from their sight. He put a comforting arm around her shoulders and guided her back through the swing doors. 'All anyone can do is hope for the best.'

'Can we go to Francine now? If she's awake I can

tell her I've seen the baby.' In spite of the warmth of his arm, Vicky's teeth were chattering and her feet were frozen from standing on the bare concrete. But it was worth it, even for such a short glimpse of the latest addition to the Latimer family.

'She'll probably sleep right through till morning,' Joe warned. 'She's on a drip for pain relief and we're putting blood in as fast as we dare. Thank goodness she's common or garden O-positive.'

'What percentage of the placenta had abrupted by the time you opened her up?' Now that the immediate danger was over Vicky was hungry for details.

'Over fifty per cent,' he said grimly, shocking her anew.

It was probably a good thing that she'd had no idea just how bad the situation had been when she'd been trying to talk to Francine. She'd probably have been too panic-struck to marshal her thoughts, let alone formulate an argument.

'I wouldn't like to do another one of those in a hurry,' he continued with heavy emphasis. 'There wasn't a single second to spare or we would definitely have lost one or both of them on the table.'

She shuddered, trying to shut her mind to just how close she had come to losing a dear friend.

On an impulse she grabbed his arm and pulled him to a halt.

'Joe, I don't know how I'll ever be able to thank you enough for what you did tonight. I've known Francine since we were little. We started school together and her family means as much to me as if we *were* family.'

'And I wouldn't have been able to do anything if you hadn't persuaded her to change her mind,' he countered equally fervently. 'I tried to tell her about the risks she was running but she was adamant that she wouldn't let me take the baby.' He closed his eyes on an expression of agony. 'I know it's the patient's right to choose to refuse treatment but it makes me feel so damned helpless when I know I should be doing something for them.'

'I'll admit she was a real hard nut to crack,' Vicky sighed, sensing that she'd just glimpsed part of Joe's own personal hell but also knowing that this was neither the time nor the place to ask him about it. 'She's been vehemently anti-abortion from the first day she understood what the word meant.'

'But I wasn't trying to *kill* the baby—I was trying to save it,' he exclaimed, clearly still frustrated by his inability to get the message across.

'That's logic, and Francine was running on her emotions—a cocktail of fear and a mother's protective instincts towards her baby, made all the more potent by a rapid loss of blood and the accompanying lack of oxygen to her brain. She wasn't in any state to think logically.'

'Well, you certainly pulled out all the stops to get her to see sense,' he said with a hint of that wicked grin lightening his eyes. 'You couldn't see it, but you had hardened old battleaxes in tears when you asked Francine for her last messages to her husband and sons.'

'I know it was melodramatic, but it was all I could think of to bring the seriousness of her situation home to her,' Vicky admitted slightly shamefacedly. 'I know how much she loves them and I used it against her.'

'Don't apologise,' he ordered as he started walking

again, this time shortening his stride so that she could easily keep pace. 'If she holds it against you, at least you can console yourself that she's *alive* to hold the grudge!'

Vicky gave a watery chuckle and realised that she was very close to overload herself. With all the events of the last few weeks, the last thing she'd needed had been to come close to losing the closest friend she had in the world.

They stopped just inside the door of Francine's room and waited while the nurse specialling her took the latest set of observations.

'She's doing well,' she murmured with a smile on her way out. 'Started complaining already.'

'Vicky,' came a croaky voice from the bed and she hurried forward.

'Francine. You're awake!' she exclaimed, marvelling at the recuperative powers of the human body.

'Nearly,' Francine croaked, and reached for Vicky's hand, tugging until she sat on the edge of the bed not draped with wires and tubes.

'Tell me the truth,' she demanded with weak tears in her eyes as she began to cry. 'Tell me what happened to my b-baby.'

'Oh, Francine, she's alive,' Vicky said with a watery smile of her own, careful not to dislodge the monitor clipped to her friend's finger as she squeezed her hand.

'Don't lie to me, Vicky,' she wailed then sobbed brokenheartedly. 'He's d-dead, isn't he? Because of m-me, my little boy d-died.'

'No. You're wrong, Francine,' Vicky said insistently, urgently trying to get through to her. 'I've seen her. She's very small, but she's going to be beautiful.'

There was a muffled conversation going on in the doorway as Joe spoke to someone outside, but Vicky was far too concerned with convincing her friend that she hadn't lost her child to wonder what else was going on in the room.

'Here,' Joe said, suddenly standing right behind her and holding out his hand to offer something to Francine. 'Will you believe this?'

Vicky recognised one of the instant photos that the unit was in the habit of taking shortly after each birth, and marvelled that someone had actually remembered to take one in such fraught circumstances.

'She was stark naked, so you can see we got the gender right,' he pointed out with a grin. 'And she was having a darned good attempt at shouting at us for taking her out of her nice warm nest, so you can see she was alive.'

Francine was so transfixed by the image she was seeing that she made no attempt to hold the photo, her grip tightening on Vicky's hand instead.

'She's mine?' she whispered in disbelief, tears still running silently down her cheeks. 'My baby girl?'

'Yes,' Vicky promised. 'She's yours.'

'And she's alive?' Her eyes lifted briefly to meet Joe's before staring back at the picture.

'She's small and it's going to be a long hard road before you can take her home, but when we sent her off to the neonatal unit she was well and truly alive.'

Francine drew in a shuddering breath and burst into a fresh deluge of noisy sobs. 'I want Andy,' she wailed. 'I want my boys.'

CHAPTER SEVEN

'I'M SHATTERED!' Vicky groaned as she slumped back into the passenger seat of Joe's car. 'I was only looking after three little boys until they fell asleep. I can't imagine how you must be feeling after operating under pressure.'

'I think I got the easier job,' he joked as he set off out of Edenthwaite. 'Those boys could show Torquemada a thing or two about interrogation techniques. And they were watching cartoons at the same time!'

'That's par for the course with Luke and Jake. They're real live wires,' Vicky said fondly. 'Heaven only knows how Francine is going to keep up with four of them. It's a good job the boys have started to go to school part time.'

'You're very close to them, aren't you?' he said quietly.

'I'm their honorary aunt, and proud of it. It means I get to do all the fun things with them, then return them to Francine hopelessly hyped up just in time for bed.'

Joe chuckled. 'Every mother's worst nightmare. I suppose you're looking forward to having a brood of your own some day, or would the position of honorary aunt be enough for you?'

'I'd love to have some of my own,' she said fervently, and was suddenly struck with the image of a little boy with his father's changeable hazel eyes and a mischievous smile. Was there any chance that he might one day exist?

Tiredness loosened her control of her tongue.

'How about you, Joe? Have you got plans in the future for a wife and family?'

He was silent for so long that Vicky had begun to think that he wasn't going to answer. His voice was chillingly expressionless when he did.

'No. No plans,' he said briefly, his tone enough to discourage any further questions. Then, out of the blue he went on bitterly, 'As the saying goes, been there, done that, got the T-shirt, done the jig-saw. I won't be doing it again.'

'What, never?' she said on a gasp. That was something Denison Memorial's grapevine didn't know. She'd noticed more than one single woman casting her eyes his way even if Joe hadn't.

And why did his absolute certainty make her feel as if he'd just betrayed her? It was ridiculous when he'd made her no promises, but she'd been so sure that there was a special awareness between them.

'Marriage is all very well but it's the rest of it that isn't worth the candle,' he said heavily in a voice that told her as clearly as his words that he had no intention of doing it again.

Vicky subsided, almost stunned with the sudden realisation that there was going to be no happy-ever-after in her life after all.

She'd thought she'd been in love with Nick, but once she'd met Joe and had got to know him, she'd realised the world of difference between an over-blown infatuation and what she felt for the man beside her in the car.

Her passion for Nick had endured through nearly

fourteen years of turbulence until she'd come to her senses. Her feelings towards Joe would probably go with her for the rest of her life and beyond.

'What time do you have to be at the hospital in the morning?' he asked as he drew up outside her cottage.

'I'm not sure. Why?' She wasn't sure of anything much beyond the growing pain around her heart. Joe was close enough that she could reach across the few inches and touch him but as far as his heart was concerned, they might as well have lived at the opposite ends of the earth.

'Because you need a lift in,' he reminded her patiently. 'Your car is waiting for some attention in the morning, remember?'

'Was that today? It seems as if years have passed since then,' she said with a puzzled shake of her head.

She forced herself to concentrate, picturing the duty roster in her mind.

'I'm on a late,' she announced when she'd sorted it out. 'I don't start my shift till one but I like to get there by at least twelve-thirty. I can always get a taxi if it's inconvenient.'

'Barring unforeseen problems, I should be finished with morning surgery by twelve. If it's any different, I'll call you in time for you to make alternative arrangements.'

How professional and efficient he sounded, as though they were merely colleagues; as if there'd never been any awareness between them, no sweet gentle brush of his lips over hers.

This time he didn't even escort her to her door, apparently content to sit in the car and watch while she let herself in. She raised her hand in thanks but she wasn't even sure he waited long enough to see it.

Vicky was too tired to eat, completely drained by the emotional overload of the day, but that didn't mean that she could sleep.

For hours she tossed and turned, her thoughts circling round first one topic then another. It seemed impossible that just a few months ago she'd been bored with the everlasting *sameness* of her life. It had seemed as if she'd spent all her time working or studying or doing household chores and there had been no end in sight.

Then she'd met Nick again and she seemed to have been caught up in a whirlwind ever since. Today it had reached tornado force, with one emotionally draining complication after another.

The flowers on her doorstep this morning had been bad enough, but they had paled into insignificance against the vandalism to her car.

Then there had been her fear that she was going to have to watch her best friend die, and the strain of having to harangue her out of her firmly held convictions so that she would allow Joe to help her. The fact that both mother and baby had survived so far was testament not only to Joe's skill but also to the capriciousness of luck.

But it was the ongoing situation with Joe that had her shedding silent tears—if it could be called ongoing. That journey home in his car could almost have been taken with a complete stranger for all the connection there had been between the two of them. It had felt almost as if he'd made a decision to cut her out of his life, even as a casual friend…and it had hurt.

It was still hurting, a huge heavy ache around her heart that sapped her energy and her happiness. It had even managed to dim her pleasure in Francine's little daughter.

Depression started to settle over Vicky like a suffocating blanket of fog until all she could see were the deficiencies in her life, the big black holes that her happiness was seeping out of like blood out of a gaping wound.

She loved her job but she'd always envisioned having something more than nursing in her life and someone to share that life with. For too many years that someone had been Nick, but she honestly didn't regret the fact that their wedding had never happened. Their marriage would probably have been happy enough, but now that she'd met Joe she knew that it would always have lacked that special touch of magic.

Losing Nick had been sad in its own way, but not as devastating as the prospect of losing Joe. Beside that, everything else paled into insignificance. Even the man who was pestering her with phone calls and damaging her car didn't matter in the overall scheme of things, as long as she knew Joe was going to be there for her.

Vicky sighed heavily, wondering at the logic in having one man so obsessed with her that he wouldn't leave her alone while the one she wanted didn't want to have anything to do with her.

Or was that true?

Vicky found herself holding her breath as she explored that idea.

Joe had been willing to act as her buffer against wagging tongues at Nick's and Frankie's wedding and even as her escort to the barn dance. If he really hadn't wanted to have anything to do with her, would he have agreed to her suggestions? Would he have stayed by her side so assiduously during the reception and danced every dance with her at the fundraiser?

Then there had been that kiss.

Well, it had probably been far too fleeting to be called a kiss, but it had definitely been initiated by Joe. He wouldn't have done *that* if he hadn't wanted to, would he?

And what about that strange feeling of awareness between them? That sensation that there was some sort of energy, some sort of elemental connection that joined the two of them whenever they touched, whenever their eyes met?

He probably didn't know that she'd seen his reaction to it, but as she'd never felt anything like it before, she'd been more aware of it when it had happened. And he had reacted, just as strongly as she had.

So why was he trying to pretend to be unaffected? Why was he deliberately putting barriers between them? Did it have something to do with his wife? Was he still in love with her? Didn't he want anyone to take her place, or was it that he just didn't want to admit that anyone *could* take her place?

The more questions she posed, the lighter the fog of depression grew.

'I *haven't* been imagining things,' she said with a new quiet confidence, a little bubble of hope lifting her spirits still higher. 'There *is* something special between us and we won't know what it is or what it could become unless we explore it.'

The only problem was going to be persuading Joe, especially if he thought he had a cast-iron reason for steering clear of any relationships.

'Should I confront him and demand some answers?' she mused, then smiled into the darkness when her mind threw up an old childhood image of the expression 'bearding the lion in his den'.

Not that Joe reminded her of a lion. He wasn't the laid-back king-of-the-savannah type with a harem of wives—he was more like the lean, dark and solitary panther.

And that could make any confrontation a dangerous prospect. If he was an injured beast, as she suspected, it could make him lash out defensively and inflict mortal wounds.

Perhaps instead of questioning him openly about his unilateral decision it would be better if she tried to use some feminine wiles?

Feminine wiles? She snorted inelegantly into the darkness. What feminine wiles? She hadn't had enough practice to know whether she had any. Her expertise was mainly in turning men away rather than trying to attract them. With her long blonde hair and blue eyes and her naturally slender figure she'd had more than one man pursuing her as though he were afraid he was going to die of testosterone poisoning if he didn't bed her immediately.

The boot was on the other foot as far as Joe was concerned and she wasn't certain she had the first idea how to go about changing his mind.

First things first, she decided logically. Start with friendship and work up. And that meant swallowing any last remnants of the hurt his change in attitude had inflicted on her today and pretending that they didn't exist. When she saw him tomorrow—and she would make certain that she saw him, tomorrow and every day after—she would smile and be friendly as though everything was all right between them.

Then, when she'd lulled his fears that she was going to want too much from him, she'd bring out the big guns—she'd ask Francine for some of the sure-fire tips that her best friend had been trying to pass on ever since they'd put on their first training bras and realised that boys were an alien race.

'Good afternoon, Joe,' she said brightly when their paths crossed for the first time the next day.

She'd half expected the phone call to tell her that he wasn't going to be able to take her to the hospital. What she didn't know was whether he'd genuinely been snowed under with work. He could have chickened out of spending time with her in the close proximity of a car even though it would only have been for a few minutes.

What he didn't know was that she'd already recruited a very willing Francine to help her. A quick phone call when Joe left her friend's room had been enough for an anxiously waiting Vicky to 'just happen' to be in the vicinity.

'How's Francine?'

'She seems to be doing well if you don't count her insistence that she's ready to leave hospital.'

'She just wants to get out of here because she can't wait to go and visit the baby.' Vicky hoped her grandmother had been wrong about the penalties of pulling faces. If the wind changed she was going to be permanently stuck with an inane grin plastered across her face. Mind you, Joe wouldn't be doing much better. He'd opted for the completely expressionless look.

'Have you heard? They've called her Amy.'

'Did she tell you why she chose the name?' For the first time her smile felt natural. She even managed a chuckle.

'Was there a special reason?' Joe actually relaxed enough to lean one shoulder against the wall.

'Right from when she was little she's always said that when she got married she wasn't going to have any boy babies, just two beautiful little girls and their names were going to be Amy and Araminta.'

'Good grief, did she ever get it wrong!' he exclaimed with a laugh.

It was only a brief laugh, but it was a start, Vicky resolved silently.

'I'm just grateful that she chose to call that little mite Amy. She's far too tiny for a name like Araminta.'

When he made his farewells Vicky was tempted to find some reason to prolong their meeting, but she forced herself to let him go with a cheery farewell of her own. This wasn't going to be a campaign aimed at a speedy solution. These meetings were hopefully going to form the foundation for a lifetime together. There was no point in hurrying things along no matter how impatient she became.

'So?' Francine demanded as soon as Vicky entered her room. 'I heard you talking, *and* laughing,' she added pointedly.

'I was telling him how long you've been waiting to call a daughter Amy.'

Francine groaned theatrically. 'I bet you told him about Araminta, and after all I've done for you. Such ingratitude!'

Vicky couldn't look penitent if she tried. It was just

so wonderful to see her friend looking so good. When she remembered how awful she'd looked last night…

'You're looking so much better,' she said quietly, silently sending up thanks for Joe's skill. 'Have you forgiven me for bullying you?'

Francine held out her hand to beckon Vicky closer. 'To be perfectly honest, a lot of last night is very hazy. I don't remember much after that idiot came round the corner on my side of the road. I was trying to steer as close to the edge of the road as I could to give him enough room to correct his steering but I must have clipped the stone wall. The police told me a witness saw the car roll twice before it stopped.'

'You're lucky to be alive, all of you,' Vicky exclaimed. She hadn't realised that the accident had been quite so serious, especially as all three children seemed to have walked away from it without a scratch.

'Me more than most,' Francine admitted. 'Andy nearly went ballistic when he heard that I nearly bled to death because I wouldn't let anyone help me. My only defence is that I wasn't thinking clearly, but you soon got my brains working again.'

'It's all part of the service,' Vicky said lightly, deliberately using humour to leaven the weight of emotion. 'Anyway, I had to make sure you survived. It would take me years to find a best friend as good as you.'

'So, does that mean you're not just looking for a friend when you're deliberately bumping into Dr Joe?' she asked pointedly. 'Come on. Spill the beans. A cryptic phone call asking for a tip-off deserves an explanation.'

In spite of the fact that they'd been friends for so

many years, Vicky was surprised to find that she was too embarrassed to admit to the full extent of her attraction to Joe.

After all, Francine had been the one who had heard all about Nick's sterling qualities ad nauseam, and the engagement had only been broken a matter of weeks ago. Would her friend think she was completely fickle if she confessed the depth of her feelings for Joe, or would she understand that it was *because* of her feelings for Nick that she now knew that her attraction towards Joe was the real thing?

'Actually, I'm hoping that he'll accept me as a friend—for starters.'

'Oho! Do I sense a romance in the offing?' Francine teased. 'He is rather good-looking in a slightly brooding sort of way. How does he feel about you?'

'Ambivalent,' Vicky said cryptically, making Francine groan.

'Facts, girl. I want facts,' she demanded. 'Are you on the rebound? I take it he knows about Nick—well, he could hardly help it when he's working in the same GP practice. Are you just after him for his gorgeous body or is there a bigger agenda?'

It was Vicky's turn to groan.

'Talk about going for the jugular! No, I'm not on the rebound. It was actually getting to know Joe that made me realise that Nick and I were making a mistake. The fact that Nick had come to the same conclusion was such an enormous relief. Anyway, you already know all this. I told you when we called the engagement off.'

'But you didn't breathe a word about Dr Joe,'

Francine amended swiftly. 'And you haven't answered any of the more interesting questions.'

'And the answers, in the order you asked them, are of course and I haven't a clue.'

'Hmm. Fascinating,' Francine mused, her blue eyes very thoughtful as she watched the heat build in Vicky's face. 'I've got a funny feeling about this. It's going to be almost interesting enough for me to want to stay in hospital a bit longer just to watch what happens.'

'As if!' Vicky scoffed. 'Nothing would stop you getting out of here as soon as you can to go and visit Amy, especially not my non-existent love life.'

She rose from the side of the bed and straightened her uniform, knowing it was time to make her escape. Anyway, it was time she was going back to the ward so that her second-in-charge could go for her break.

'Anything you need when I come next time?' she offered.

'Nothing, thanks. Andy's bringing the boys in to visit later. Mum's staying with them till I'm on my feet again and you probably remember what a whiz she is at organisation.'

'I remember. You're going to be spoiled rotten, especially as you've given her an excuse to make all the frilly pink things she's always wanted to.'

Francine's eyes strayed to the photo propped up beside her on the top of the locker and her eyes instantly grew suspiciously moist.

'I'm going to be thanking you and Dr Joe for the rest of my life,' she said huskily. 'And not just because I would probably have lost that life if you hadn't intervened.'

'Don't get your hopes too high, Francine,' Vicky

cautioned, hating to dampen her friend's joy. 'She's very tiny and she's got a mountain to climb before you can even think about a future for her. Just take it one day at a time or even one minute at a time when she goes through a bad patch.'

'I might not have your medical background but I've seen enough documentaries on television to know the sort of things we're going to face,' her friend said seriously. 'I know there are dozens of things that can go wrong, but I've got a feeling deep inside that it isn't just luck that Amy's been allowed to survive. I also believe that some awful things are allowed to happen because there's a purpose to them. I'm convinced that Amy's alive because she's got a special reason to be here with us.'

Francine's words came back to Vicky at intervals over the next few days.

The idea that there could be a hidden reason behind some events wasn't a new one, but it was the first time she'd wondered if the concept could be applied to her own life.

Had there been a reason why she'd become so fixated on Nick as her future life's partner that she'd barely looked at another man? Had there been a reason why she and Joe should have met here in Denison Memorial and why he should have been the one to take pity on her when she'd been determined to show her face at Nick's and Frankie's wedding?

She would probably never know the answers, but at least the contemplation of the questions was helping her to compose her soul in patience while she waged her war of attrition against Joe's reserve.

And there *had* been a few cracks in the stony façade, such as his answering smile of pleasure when her fully repaired car had been returned to her.

'They've even cleaned it, inside and out,' she'd exclaimed as she'd examined it. 'It might almost be worth having an accident every few months just to have it returned looking this good.'

The only downside to having her own transport back was the fact that she didn't get to spend those few precious minutes with Joe when he'd given her a lift to and from work. Still, if she got desperate, Francine had pointed out that there was always the ploy of the flat battery...

She'd seen another big crack in his façade of disinterest that same afternoon. She'd gone up to visit Francine for a firsthand report of her first emotional visit to see Amy, and had found Joe giving little Paul a ride on his shoulders.

He was obviously embarrassed to be caught out playing with the toddler but Vicky found it completely endearing that such a strong silent man could blush like that and yet not stop his game.

She lost her heart to him completely the next time she visited and found him talking to Andy and Francine while cradling the sleeping child in his arms.

'He would make a wonderful father,' Francine said when he made his excuses a little while later and left with Andy and Paul so that the two friends could talk.

'You know that and I know that but he's already told me that he's not interested,' Vicky said sadly, still thrilled that her friend should have such a high opinion of the man she'd come to love.

'Was he trying to tell you he wasn't interested in being a father or wasn't interested in you?' Francine asked. 'Because I don't really believe either. He can't keep his eyes off you whenever you're in the same room, and you've seen for yourself that he can't keep his hands off Paul.'

'So where does that leave me?' Vicky demanded in frustration. 'I know what *I* want. *He's* the one who backed off.'

'I've got a feeling it leaves you with some hard decisions to make,' Francine warned, her blue eyes full of sympathy.

'Such as?' Even as she spoke Vicky knew that the question was only a delaying tactic. She already knew what Francine was going to say.

'Well, we both know that you've always intended to marry and have children, but what if you're faced with an option? What if you're faced with a choice of having either one or the other but not both?'

'You mean, what if I've got to decide between having the family I've always wanted and having Joe?' Vicky said, finally coming down to the nitty-gritty. 'And for all the fact that he's not disappearing in the other direction any more when he sees me, he certainly hasn't come *close* to indicating that he's willing to start a relationship.'

'If you'd seen the expression in his eyes you wouldn't have any doubts about his willingness,' Francine informed her with a salacious grin, but then grew serious again. 'You know, I've got a feeling that there's more to his wariness than the simple surface stuff.'

'Such as?' Vicky challenged again, hoping Francine might come up with something she hadn't already agonised over.

'Well, it could be the difference in your ages...'

'Francine! I can't believe you're saying that!

There's more years between you and Andy than there are between Joe and I.'

'I'm not saying that *I* think it's a problem,' Francine corrected her smartly. 'I'm saying it might be a problem for him. After all, he's so sombre sometimes that he probably comes over as older than his chronological age, while you still look little older than a teenager. He's probably afraid people will think he's a cradle-snatcher.'

'Well, thanks for the backhanded compliment!' Vicky complained in exasperation. 'So what would I have to do? Wear a placard around my neck saying 'HE'S ONLY THIRTY-SEVEN AND I'M TWENTY-SIX' every time we go out together?'

'It wouldn't be necessary,' Francine said quietly. 'You haven't seen how much younger he looks when he's talking about you. Anyway, you'd soon age a decade or two by the time you'd had a few babies— Ah!' She brought herself up short when she realised what she'd said.

'We're back to the either-or scenario again,' Vicky said with hard-won resignation.

'And I'm beginning to wonder if everything's somehow connected to something in his past.' There was a questioning lift to Francine's brows but Vicky ignored the prompt. She just nodded thoughtfully without revealing her own fears on that score.

Francine might be her best friend but Joe had told her about his wife in confidence. She hadn't breathed a word even though she was privately becoming convinced that Francine might have hit the nail on the head.

She was still thinking about it when she started her shift. She'd already spent days wondering what she was going to do to find out the answers without putting the new, more relaxed rapport between herself and Joe at risk. Her latest deliberations were interrupted rudely by a call from Accident and Emergency warning her that she had a patient arriving in a minute.

'She's in her fifties and comatose,' the voice on the other end of the phone warned her.

'Comatose!' Vicky exclaimed in surprise.

'Before you say anything, I know you haven't got the set-up or the staff numbers to deal with long-term high-dependency nursing,' he said hastily. 'This is just a stopgap measure until we know what's going on, and we haven't got anywhere else to put her. The locum was called out to her last night and arrived to find her in a bad way. At first glance it looks as if she's had a heart attack and we've started treatment on that supposition, but it doesn't look good. We've taken bloods and directed the results to come back to you. Depending on what they show, she might have to be transferred for the high-dependency nursing.'

Even though the prospect of nursing her was going to be a logistical nightmare, Vicky half hoped that the poor woman's condition wouldn't necessitate sending her to the city. It made visiting so much more difficult for family members.

That wasn't something that she could do anything about. Getting her precious single-bedded room prepared for its new occupant was, and any further contemplation of her relationship with Joe was going to have to wait until she had a moment to breathe— probably in the few seconds before she fell asleep and dreamed about him.

CHAPTER EIGHT

VICKY was heavy-hearted when, before she had even reached the department, the patient on her way up from Accident and Emergency suddenly died.

'There'll have to be a post-mortem, of course,' said Mrs Olsen knowledgeably, looking up from the knitting that was never far from her hand.

She'd been the life and soul of the ward ever since she'd arrived and Vicky had noticed that she had very quickly tapped into the hospital grapevine via a second cousin's son who was one of the porters. Marjorie Olsen almost seemed to know what was going on before the staff did.

When Vicky made no comment to her prediction of a post-mortem, the cheery woman continued to chatter undeterred.

'We had to have one for my mother. Healthy as a horse she was, and still with all her marbles in spite of the fact she was over eighty. Apparently she had a bit of a fall just after I came into hospital and when the doctor arrived he said she'd had a heart attack. He did what he could for her but she'd already died by the time she got to the hospital. It was just after my operation and I had to go to the funeral in a wheelchair but I couldn't have missed it, could I? Not when she'd been such a wonderful mother.'

Silently, Vicky marvelled that Mrs Olsen seemed to be able to talk for ever without even drawing breath.

'Of course, we were almost expecting it,' she continued, unabated. 'Just a couple of days earlier, before I came into hospital, her closest friend went exactly the same way. Well, not exactly because she didn't have a fall. Hers was a touch of the bronchitics hanging on after the winter, and Mother phoned for the doctor because her friend was having difficulty breathing.'

Vicky tried to interrupt so that she could make a start on checking the drugs cupboard but it would have been easier to stop a juggernaut with a feather.

'Ever so nice he was,' Mother said. 'He's that new doctor in the practice out at the other end of the valley. You know the one I mean—towards the big motorway junction. He tried to help her, gave her a big injection, but there wasn't really anything he could do. Mother said she went all sweaty and trembly and her mind was all confused and then she had a fit and went unconscious. That must have been when her heart stopped, because when the ambulance came they said she was dead.

'I just hope it was as quick for Mother. She'd lived all on her own ever since Father passed on and there would have been no one to help her if the doctor hadn't come as quickly as he did, not with me in hospital and my John out on the farm somewhere.'

Vicky resigned herself to having to wait until the story reached a natural conclusion, if it ever did.

'Terry said—he's our Sandra's boy that works as a porter here—he said there's always several of the older folks that dies in the winter, but it's still going on in our village, even though spring's here. Soon there'll be none left and then *we'll* be the older generation.'

The arrival of the tea-trolley finally signalled release but Vicky found herself puzzling over something that was niggling at the back of her mind. There was something that Marjorie Olsen had said, or referred to, or had jogged her memory.

Unfortunately, it seemed to be one of those things that the harder you tried to grasp them, the further they slipped out of reach.

She was still distracted when the phone rang. Without thinking, she picked it up.

There had been no more calls from her stalker—in fact, no contact of any kind for several days—so it was a real shock to hear that taunting voice again.

'Victoria,' he said in that habitual singsong voice, then added in the same tone, 'I'm still here…' It set every hair on the back of her neck standing on end.

For one blinding second she was tempted to scream something very rude down the phone, but Joe had warned her that could trigger an escalation in the stalker's activities.

The last thing she wanted was for him to come any closer than he had already, so she held her tongue. She didn't want to listen to him, and had no intention of speaking, but slamming the phone down could only serve to anger him. All she could do was focus, not so much on what he was saying but on the slightest sound she might hear in the background—anything that might give her a clue who was doing this to her.

At first all she could hear was the empty crackle of an open phone line, but gradually she picked out other things. There was a distant hollow tick-tock, as if there was a grandfather clock on the other side of the room, and even further away a quick burst of something that sounded like birdsong.

She didn't know how long she sat there with the phone to her ear, but the last thing she wanted to hear was his final words as he broke the connection.

'Right, that's it!' Joe exclaimed angrily. 'You're phoning the police—now!'

'But, Joe, what can they do?' she protested. 'Be logical.'

'Logical is the last thing I'm feeling at the moment,' he growled as he prowled backwards and forwards in the cramped office, his resemblance to a panther more marked than ever.

When she'd told him that the man had been in contact again he'd been angry enough, but when she repeated his 'I'll be seeing you' message, Joe had looked as if he'd been about to erupt.

'The police could make sure that the bastard doesn't come anywhere near you,' he declared heatedly.

'And how would they do that?' she asked sweetly, inwardly revelling in the overwhelming evidence of his concern. Was it just compassion for a fellow human being or did his feelings for her go deeper than either of them had realised? 'How many police do you think they have available to act as twenty-four-hour bodyguards?'

'That's not the point,' he argued as he reached for the phone. 'We've already seen what sort of damage he can do to a car. I'm not waiting to see what he does to you.'

Vicky subsided, realising that she wasn't going to win this battle.

While she listened to Joe working his way up through the various layers of officialdom she reflected on the change in his attitude towards her. For all that she'd been completely independent ever since she'd left home to begin her nursing training, she had to admit that it felt wonderful to have someone who was concerned about her safety.

It was especially wonderful that it was Joe. It almost made it worthwhile being stalked if his apprehension had kick-started him into caring about her on a personal level.

'They're sending someone to the hospital to talk to you,' he announced in a satisfied voice as he put the phone down. 'They should be here before long.'

'But I'm working, Joe. I can't take time off from my duties to talk to a policeman.'

'I don't think you'll find anyone complaining. They're going to want to have a word with Marc Fletcher about hospital security. As manager, he should know that the provision of supervision for the staff parking areas isn't stringent enough. What if that lunatic who slit your tyres had still been waiting there with the knife?'

'Well, yes, but—'

'And it's not just you and the other nurses. There are a lot of vulnerable people in and around Denison Memorial. It's not safe to have someone like that on the loose, not when we don't know how far he's willing to go.'

Vicky shuddered. She wouldn't admit it to Joe, but secretly she was glad that he and the police were taking the matter seriously. Ever since the episode with her tyres she'd been dreading the end of each shift, wondering what other nasty shocks she might find when she went out to her car. At least when he'd been

giving her lifts to and from work she hadn't had to
worry.

The trouble was, she didn't want to appear as if
she needed looking after. She was a well-qualified
professional with a responsible job, and she wanted
Joe to see her that way. Francine was concerned that
the difference in their ages might be a factor in his
determination not to allow any involvement between
them, and any hint that she was too feeble to take
care of herself might militate against her in her campaign to win him over.

She drew in a deep breath and released it slowly,
counting silently to ten. She was so cross that she
could have chewed penny nails and spat carpet tacks,
as her grandmother used to say.

She'd begun to think that this stalker might have
got bored with her lack of hysteria and given up on
her. Now, just when she'd felt she might be making
a bit of headway against Joe's wariness, everything
was in turmoil again and he was seeing her as someone who needed looking after rather than as a potential partner.

It was obvious that Joe had every intention of waiting to meet the officer and putting in his two pennies'
worth, but he was thwarted by a call taking him down
to the accident and emergency department.

'It sounds as if this may take some time,' he said
crossly when he put the phone down. 'A skateboarder
misjudged the edge of the pavement and put his arm
through a shop window.'

Vicky didn't know whether she was relieved when
he left or not. If he didn't hear her admit how scared
she was by the whole situation she was going to be
able to maintain her façade of capability in front of

him. On the other hand, there was a definite feeling of safety when he was nearby which she missed as soon as he was out of sight. Even the knowledge that he was only a phone call away wasn't the same.

When the officer finally arrived Vicky realised that she was just as guilty of gender stereotyping as the next person. She'd expected to have to deal with a man in a smart uniform who would probably dismiss her fears as nothing more than female hysteria. What she got was a pretty woman not much older than herself who was only too willing to understand how unnerving it was to be stalked.

The interview took a slightly disjointed hour, with Vicky having to break off at odd intervals to answer important questions from one or other of her junior staff.

They ended the session with a refill of the teapot and a few minutes of commiseration about the various problems encountered by women in the workplace.

'Life is one long nightmare at the moment,' WPC Ducci admitted wearily. 'My husband's gone back home to Italy to decide whether he loves me enough to put up with English weather and my mother died suddenly from a heart attack. She was actually in the doctor's surgery and he did what he could for her, but it was too severe for her to survive. It was such a shock because she'd never told me she was being treated for a heart problem or I'd never have asked her to look after my daughter when she came out of school before my shift ended.'

Vicky always felt it was rather like walking a tightrope, finding the right words to say in such situations.

'At least you know she was in the right place to be treated quickly,' she offered.

'Her doctor was wonderful,' she said with a smile. 'He's much younger than Mum's usual one. A locum, I think, but he took the time to tell me that he'd made sure she hadn't suffered.'

Something was niggling at the back of Vicky's memory again. How many times had she heard about that new locum and how wonderful he was? And how many times had she heard it in connection with an older patient suffering an unexpected heart attack?

Don't be silly, she admonished herself. You're so worked up about this stalker that you're seeing criminals everywhere. Still, she couldn't help asking, 'What was the name of this doctor? Was he one from the GP unit at Denison Memorial?'

'No. He's from the practice at the other end of the valley, closer to the motorway junction. Quite good-looking, too, if you're single and interested. His name is Naismith. Have you come across him?'

'Briefly, when he called in to check up on a patient he'd admitted.' A patient who'd been dead on arrival after suffering a fatal heart attack, if she remembered rightly. 'And I may be single, but I'm not interested.'

'Ah,' the police officer said with a knowing smile. 'Got your sights set on someone, have you? Take my advice and take your time to get to know the man before you leap into marriage. I met Gino on holiday one year, and by the time twelve months were up we were married and our daughter had been born.'

'Chance would be a fine thing,' Vicky muttered with a careful glance around for potential eavesdroppers. 'I'm already certain, but if he had his way we'd never move beyond platonic friendship.'

'Well, you wouldn't be doing this job if you didn't enjoy a challenge, so my money's on you,' Angela

Ducci said encouragingly. 'Hopefully, all this nasti-
ness will blow over and the next time I hear about
you it will be seeing a picture of your wedding in the
local paper.'

Vicky just laughed, but as she showed the police-
woman out she wondered just how likely that was.

At least it was good to know that she'd been doing
the right things in dealing with the stalking pest, and
WPC Ducci had given her plenty of tips and good
advice gleaned from other women's experiences.

'So, what did she say?' Joe demanded.

The surprise of hearing his voice right behind her
nearly sent Vicky into orbit.

'Don't *do* that!' she snapped, wondering if she'd
just broken all records for the world's fastest heart
rate. Mind you, it probably wouldn't have been much
different if she'd seen him coming. He had that sort
of effect on her pulse every time.

'Sorry to startle you but I thought you'd heard me
come in. I take it the police have come and gone.'

'Some time ago,' she confirmed briefly. 'How did
your patchwork go?'

He grimaced. 'He was very lucky that he hadn't
damaged anything major, although how he'd avoided
it I'll never know, seeing the mess he was in. It took
dozens of stitches to put it all back together. So, what
are they going to do?'

'Who? Do about what?'

'The police, about your stalker,' he said impatiently. 'Are they organising some protection for
you?'

'Hardly,' Vicky scoffed. 'You read the papers and
watch the news. If they haven't got the manpower to

provide protection for battered wives and abused children, they're unlikely to be able to produce it out of
a hat for me.'

'So what are they going to do? They can't just
wash their hands of it, not when the incidents have
been escalating.' Joe rammed the fingers of one hand
through his thick, dark hair, leaving it uncharacteris-
tically ruffled. Was the light catching on the first silvery strands or was it just an illusion? His outburst
certainly bore all the fervour of a young man, as did
his agitated pacing.

In fact, it was quite flattering how hot he was getting under the collar on her behalf, but it wasn't
achieving anything.

'How about a cup of tea while I tell you all about
it?' she suggested, guessing it was probably the only
course to take if she wanted him to calm down some
time this century. At least she could censor what she
told him without him being any the wiser.

'Right,' she began, when they were both sitting
with steaming mugs and an open tin of biscuits between them. 'WPC Ducci said that, thanks to your
advice, I'd been doing all the right things so far.
Keeping everything calm and non-confrontational,
that is. She's sending someone—I think it was something like crime awareness—to advise Marc about
personnel safety around the hospital. It will probably
mean extra lights around the parking areas and
closed-circuit television cameras to keep an eye on
what's going on out there.'

'But that won't be done overnight,' Joe pointed out
swiftly.

'True, and that's why she recommended that I
should make sure I always have company when I

walk out to my car. With someone like that around, she said it would be a good policy for all the women on the staff—at least until the security's been beefed up.'

'What else did she say? What about the phone calls?'

'Apparently the British telephone system, once they have police authorisation, can trace any number that calls me. Provided the caller isn't using an illegally cloned mobile, that should give them the number of the caller and, therefore, his name.'

'It sounds almost too simple, but will it work when your calls are going through the hospital switchboard? How can they separate the guilty ones from all the other ones you get in a day?'

'I didn't bother asking for all the technical details,' she confessed. 'All I was interested in was how they were going to stop this man from stalking me and how they're going to catch him so he can't put anyone else through this either.'

'So, what did the WPC say about the flower delivery to your cottage? Do you need to have a camera set up there, too?'

'She asked if I had anyone who would be willing to stay with me for a while, but I'm reluctant to drag anyone else into this. I'd never forgive myself if they got hurt because they got between me and the stalker.'

'That's all very noble, but I think you're missing the point,' he butted in impatiently. 'In his last message he said he was going to see you soon and, having seen what he did to your car, I don't like the idea of you being in that house alone. I think you should move in with me until the police can catch him.'

He made it sound so simple, but just the thought

of moving in with Joe was enough to scramble her brain.

It was tempting. Very tempting.

The idea of getting up each morning in his house and having breakfast together then going home with him each night to share a meal. It would be only one step removed from living together like husband and wife.

Unfortunately, it wasn't a feasible idea, not least because she probably wouldn't be able to remain sane if she were to live in such close proximity to him for any length of time while they still had a platonic relationship. But if they were lovers…

No, this was neither the time nor the place to think about that. Tonight she would lie in bed and mourn the chance she was turning down.

'It's a very generous offer, but if the police are going to have a chance to catch the stalker I've got to be somewhere where he can try to make contact. They've got to have some means of tracking him, and if I just disappear…'

'You mean you're *deliberately* leaving yourself vulnerable?' Joe interrupted, only just remembering in time to tone his voice down from a roar of disbelief. 'You're actually hoping that he'll keep pestering you so the police have a chance to catch him in the act?'

'What would you suggest?' she challenged. 'I can hardly go into hiding, can I? It would be a little difficult to earn my living. Anyway,' she continued, not giving him a chance to interrupt again, 'I refuse to let someone like that dictate how I'm going to live my life. He has no right.'

Joe's lips were pressed tightly together, as if he was

barely keeping angry words inside, but it was the expression of concern in his eyes that turned Vicky's insides to warm honey.

'Joe, I promise I won't take any chances,' she said, deliberately softening her tone.

'But you will be,' he growled fiercely. 'Just by setting yourself up like this, by making it possible for him to contact you, you leave yourself open to be hurt.'

'There isn't really any other choice,' she said, trying to use logic to sway him to her way of thinking. She needed to know that she could call on him if she needed help, or even a little extra reassurance. 'I'd never forgive myself if, because he couldn't stalk me any more, he turned on someone who didn't have the sort of backup I can call on in Denison Memorial.'

He made a wordless sound that told her he still wasn't happy about it, but she had a feeling that at least he understood her reasoning now.

'What I can't understand is why he targeted me in the first place,' she said suddenly, her late night heart-searching and deliberation emerging into speech. 'I mean, it's not as if I'm any sort of celebrity like a Hollywood actress or a pop star or the daughter of a millionaire, so why me?'

'You're not serious, are you?' Joe laughed in disbelief. 'Don't you ever look in the mirror, Vicky? You're a stunningly beautiful young woman, all long legs, long blonde hair and blue eyes. And as if that weren't enough, you're hard-working, good at your job and you've got a wonderful caring nature.'

Embarrassment at so much praise had her blushing furiously. Did he think she'd been fishing for compliments that he'd supplied so many?

'You make me sound too good to be true, but if that were the case I wouldn't have got to twenty-six and still been on the shelf.'

'Twenty-six?' There was an arrested look on his face and he was looking at her as if he'd never seen her before.

'Very nearly twenty-seven,' she confirmed. 'Almost time to put a deposit down on a Zimmer frame. Why? How old did you think I was?'

'Twenty-two or -three at the most…well that's how old you look to me,' he said defensively, then carried on in a musing tone, almost as if he was thinking aloud, 'But you're a ward sister, and you don't get a post like that in a place like Denison Memorial without having several years of experience under your belt.'

Vicky knew her expression must be rather smug because his own grew apologetic when he caught sight of it.

'Do I owe you an apology?' he offered quietly, with that endearing hint of darker colour edging up his throat and into the lean planes of his face.

'You mean, for treating me like a barely grown-up child rather than a woman old enough to know her own mind?' she taunted pointedly, then decided to turn the situation to her own advantage. 'Yes, you probably do owe me an apology, but I'd rather you took me out for a meal or something. Anything to take my mind off that creep.'

She shuddered at the thought that even as she did something as ordinary and innocent as going out for a meal someone could be watching her, following her…

She didn't like the feeling that her life was out of

control; that someone else could dictate what she did; that someone else was limiting her freedom and might even be planning to take her life.

Take her life…

It was only an expression but it was a chilling one, and all of a sudden it reminded her of her wild suspicion that someone might be mistreating some of their elderly patients.

'Joe—' she began, coming out of her introspection to find he'd stopped his lethal pacing to stand right in front of her.

'I think that's a good idea,' he said, but, surrounded by that indefinable mixture of antibacterial handwash, laundry soap and male musk that was unique to Joe, she'd completely lost the thread of the conversation.

'You do?' she said blankly, and blinked up at him, noticing in fascination that his eyes seemed more green than hazel today.

'Yes. Have you got any suggestions? Any preferences?'

'Preferences?' she parroted, still at a loss. And he knew it, the rat. She could tell that he was laughing at her for losing track of what he was talking about.

'Going out for a meal?' he finally reminded her with a knowing chuckle. 'What were you thinking about?'

'Actually, I was wondering how I'd go about finding out about any locum GPs in the Edenthwaite area.'

'What sort of thing do you want to know and why?'

It didn't take him long to switch gears, Vicky noticed, but, then, theirs had always been more of a business relationship rather than the more personal one she wanted.

'Basic things. Such as how many are there, how long have they been in the area, have they sent any patients into Denison Memorial and have they visited the hospital?' The list came off the top of her head. She'd probably have more questions when she discovered the numbers involved.

'Wait a minute. Where's this coming from?' he demanded. 'I don't remember you telling me anything about your stalker that would make you think he was a locum GP. Have I missed something?'

'Good Lord, no!' she exclaimed. 'This is something else entirely and I'm probably barking up the wrong tree...'

'Vicky! Spit it out!'

She gave an impatient huff, suddenly realising that she'd been rambling.

'I just want to check up to reassure myself that I'm imagining spectres, I suppose, but over the last few weeks I've heard of several older patients living in roughly the same area who've had to call a doctor out on an emergency. According to relatives and friends, they've either been found already dead when the GP arrived, or they've been DOA when he's sent them in here.'

'Vicky, unfortunately that's part of what being a GP is about—everything from birth to death—and most of us get to see more deaths than births.'

'But do all your elderly patients die of heart attacks? Are they all struck down unexpectedly?' she challenged, then softened her approach. 'As I said, I've heard about several cases recently and I just wanted your help to check it out because I'd never forgive myself if something was amiss...'

He was silent for a moment, watching her, then he gave a wry shake of his head.

'Did anyone ever tell you that you might have an overdeveloped sense of responsibility?'

There was a tap on the door and Vicky's second-in-charge stuck her head hesitantly round the edge.

'I don't know whether it's safe to interrupt or if I'm going to witness the outbreak of World War Three,' she began cheekily, 'but I'm having trouble with Marjorie Olsen's drip.'

Vicky grimaced. 'I hadn't realised we were that bad,' she apologised obliquely. 'How much could you hear on the ward?'

'Nothing, except that Dr Joe wasn't happy about something.' She grinned again at Vicky. 'You had a couple of patients ready to come in and stand up for you if he was giving you a hard time. They think he's good, but they think you can walk on water.'

'So do I slink out of here with my tail between my legs, whimpering all the way, or do I put a brave face on it and accompany Vicky onto the ward?'

'Oh, I think the brave face,' Vicky decided. 'It's much more attractive than the hangdog one and far sexier than when you go all inscrutable.'

She had a silent chuckle at the quick wash of heat that her sally brought to Joe's face, but she was only teasing him in reaction to the difference in the air between them. For the first time since she'd met him it actually felt as if he was seeing her as almost an equal, at least in the determination stakes.

Part of the blame for that was hers, she knew. It couldn't have helped her image that she'd shed tears over him a time or two. But part of the blame was his, too, for assuming things about her without making an effort to find out if they were true.

It was always thought to be a compliment for a woman to be told she looked younger than her years, but she'd never really paid much notice to her own looks. It seemed as though Francine had been right when she'd guessed that her youthful appearance had misled Joe.

The repositioning of the IV didn't take more than a minute but she could see that Joe was slightly uncomfortable throughout the procedure. Well, he probably had the feeling that all eyes were looking on critically, waiting to see if he put a foot wrong. There was definitely the air of a kangaroo court about the ward.

Luckily Joe had many years of practice to call on and an excellent bedside manner. With Marjorie Olsen as susceptible to masculine flattery as the next woman, her delighted laughter soon smoothed things over.

Vicky still felt slightly self-conscious as she followed Joe out to the hallway, but they hadn't finalised any of the topics they'd covered so heatedly in her office.

'I'll go back to the surgery and do some checking,' he volunteered before she could open her mouth. 'I'll be able to let you know what I've found out when I see you this evening. Will eight do?'

'Eight will be fine,' she agreed readily, just as the lift doors opened and Grant Naismith walked out.

'How do you want me to dress?' Joe asked suddenly, holding the doors open with one hand braced against them. Just as suddenly, his pose inspired a mental image of the man standing there without a stitch on.

'What do you mean?' Oh, it was hard to speak normally when she was having trouble reining in her imagination *and* her hormones. Had Grant read her mind? He'd certainly had a very disapproving expression on his face.

'Well, this was *your* suggestion, so I thought you were making all the decisions. Don't you usually expect your date to give you a clue where you're going so you can dress accordingly?'

She knew he was teasing and she treated the request in that vein, suggesting an Italian bistro she'd heard several colleagues recommend. At the same time, there was a little place deep inside her that was exulting, knowing that he'd almost admitted, in words of one syllable, that they were going out on a date.

CHAPTER NINE

WHAT on earth had possessed him? Joe fumed as he wrapped a tie around the collar of his shirt and proceeded to make a complete mess of tying it.

He was a thirty-seven-year-old widower, for heaven's sake. He had no right to be going out on dates, even though someone like Vicky had virtually done the asking.

Someone like Vicky? What was he thinking?

There was no one like Vicky. She was completely unique, completely stubborn and exasperating, and completely captivating.

If he had any decency left in him he would be staying as far away from her as possible. He already knew that there was no room for someone so vibrantly alive in his life, and there was no need in her life for someone who had already been once around the clock.

So why was it that when she'd suggested they go out for a meal he'd seen it as a challenge and he'd snapped at it, making arrangements for the time and the place when he could simply have ignored the idea altogether?

And there was no point trying to con himself that they needed to meet to discuss the results of his enquiries. That didn't need an intimate meal in an Italian bistro. A mug of tea in the staff lounge would have covered that, bearing in mind the innocent nature of his findings.

Perhaps the time had come for a little honesty, Joe thought uncomfortably as he met his own eyes in the mirror. It was probably overdue.

The long and the short of it was that Vicky Lawrence had fascinated him from the first day she'd joined the staff at Denison Memorial, and nothing like that had happened since he'd met Celia all those years ago when they'd been just teenagers and had married when he'd still been a raw medical student.

Vicky had obviously been a little shy about her brother's boisterous welcome and a little embarrassed about all the questions she'd had to field about her forthcoming marriage. When he'd looked up from the article he'd been reading in the latest issue of *Pulse*, he'd caught his first glimpse of that beautiful blonde hair and sweet smile and he'd imagined that the sun had just started shining.

Since then he'd done his best to ignore her but still his brain had been filing away snippets about her. Like the way she tried to keep that fly-away hair under control during her shifts by twisting it up and skewering it with pins and the way her blue eyes gleamed with laughter when she was teasing her brother.

She'd teased *him* today, and the colour of her eyes had seemed almost electric. Then there was the way she stood up to him when she disagreed with him, tilting her chin at that belligerent angle that made him want to grab her and kiss her senseless without a care for who might be watching.

It was crazy. He'd never been tempted to behave like that before and he didn't like it now. He couldn't afford to let his life spin out of control again. He'd never really recovered from the last time when he'd lost everything he'd loved by gut-wrenching inches right before his eyes.

That was the reminder he needed to bring him to his senses. All he had to do was remember the day he'd buried Celia, buried her and all the bright hopes they'd had on their wedding day.

With that firmly in mind he'd have no problem spending a pleasant evening in Vicky's company while he set her mind at rest over her potentially disastrous suspicions.

'So, tell me everything,' Vicky said, leaning forward eagerly as soon as the waiter disappeared with the menus. 'It'll probably be ages before he comes back with any food so there's no excuse.'

She couldn't take her eyes off Joe as the candlelight gilded the lean planes of his face. She'd seen him in his dark suits and his theatre scrubs and she'd whirled around a dance floor with him in well-worn jeans. Tonight he was wearing black chinos and a black shirt set off with a pewter-coloured tie, and she thought he looked a little dangerous but totally, utterly delicious.

How was she going to keep her mind on their conversation when her eyes wouldn't leave him alone?

'I thought it would be best if we didn't make any waves until we were a little more certain what we were dealing with,' he began seriously, but he was watching his hands as he toyed with his cutlery and she couldn't drag her eyes away either.

They'd both decided to start with a main course but she now almost wished that they'd opted for a starter just to have something to focus on.

'I spun a tale about gathering information for a paper I wanted to write about the availability of locums in Cumbria,' he continued. 'They were so willing to help it made me feel quite guilty, especially when they faxed me a list of those who had worked in this part of the country in the last year. They even included the names and addresses so I could contact them for their impressions and experiences.'

'And?' The fact that he'd got so far in such a short space of time had finally drawn her attention away from the man himself. She was eager to know more but dreading it at the same time. It was one thing to enjoy the intellectual exercise of tracking down information but another entirely when she realised what they might be uncovering.

At the same time she had the vague feeling that he was keeping something back from her, that he wasn't meeting her eyes because he was...what? Leading her on?

'There seem to be two completely different types of locum around. There are the family men and women or the semi-retired who make themselves available in a limited area so that they don't have to move house with each new job. Then there are those who seem to be happy to take posts over a much wider area.'

'How many of them have been sending patients to Denison Memorial?' She'd been sidetracked by the information for a moment, wondering what sort of person wouldn't want to have a home base somewhere. She should be concentrating on the information Joe had discovered.

'Only one, and it's someone you know—Grant Naismith.'

'You mean, he's the one who's been sending all

the DOAs in?' she gasped, then saw Joe shaking his head and was completely confused. She really would have to concentrate better if she wasn't going to lose the thread so easily. 'So what *are* you saying?' she demanded crossly.

'You obviously haven't been listening to the local news this evening or you'd have heard the big story.' He put on a typical newsreader's voice. 'Locum GP Grant Naismith was so concerned about his patients that he single-handedly tracked down a contaminated water supply that has been claiming the lives of some of the more vulnerable inhabitants of a Cumbrian village.'

'What? Grant?' she exclaimed, stunned and delighted by the simple answer to all her worries, then she caught sight of Joe's face. 'You rat!' she exclaimed. 'You really enjoyed leading me on, didn't you? I suppose you think I was stupid to suspect that someone could be—'

'No, Vicky,' he said quickly, covering her hand with his to quieten her. 'I don't think you're in the least stupid because you could easily have been right. You were brave to stick your neck out when you thought you'd spotted suspicious circumstances. I'm just so glad that it turned out to be natural causes rather than a rogue colleague that I couldn't resist teasing you. Will you forgive me?'

'I'll have to think about it,' she said with a scowl, knowing that she would probably forgive him almost anything if he looked at her like that.

They had to break off then to allow their waiter to set steaming plates of linguini in front of them.

Silence reigned while they tasted and then devoured the delicious sauce poured over perfectly prepared pasta.

Joe had finished his while Vicky was still struggling with half a plateful, and she couldn't help noticing the covetous eyes he was sending in her direction.

'You might as well dig in,' she invited with a grin, pushing the plate towards him so that they could both reach. 'I'm never going to be able to manage all of this, delicious though it is.'

'You're sure?' he asked, but he'd already got his fork ready in his hand. 'Does this mean you've forgiven me?'

'I'm still thinking about it,' she said with a sniff.

There was something very intimate about sharing the food that way, forks probing and clashing as they hunted out the tastiest morsels of seafood, and she couldn't help realising that this was something she'd never have dreamt of doing with Nick.

The tables were turned when it came to dessert. Vicky was too full to contemplate ordering one, but when she saw the delicious concoction placed in front of Joe she couldn't help reaching for her fork.

'Just a taste?' she pleaded, her tastebuds already craving the rich, bitter taste of all that luscious dark chocolate and the sharp sweetness of the raspberries.

To her surprise he parried her approaching utensil with his own, using it almost like a sword.

The look of wicked mischief in his eyes was priceless and made her all the more determined to steal a bite.

She failed hopelessly and her stomach was aching with laughter when he finally offered her a taste from his own fork.

Afraid that he would change his mind at the last moment, she wrapped her hand around his on the handle and leant forward with her mouth open.

She was just about to close her lips around the small mound he was offering when she glanced up at him and found his eyes fixed on her with an expression she couldn't mistake. They were so dark and so intent on what she was doing that she couldn't fail to see the desire in them.

Slowly Vicky pressed her lips together and withdrew, taking the tidbit with her and leaving the tines of the fork completely clean.

She hardly dared to chew even though Joe seemed to be waiting for her to do so. Why else would he be staring at her mouth like that? Then she saw the tip of his tongue slip out to touch his lips, and when every nerve in her body clenched in reaction to the sight she understood.

Suddenly chocolate and raspberries didn't seem nearly so interesting, not when there was the possibility of tasting Joe's lips instead. Would they taste of the heavy sweetness of the chocolate and the sharp tang of the berries? Would she have a chance to find out?

She was almost certain she heard Joe groan as he dragged his eyes away, and he seemed to have completely lost interest in finishing his dessert.

Vicky couldn't think of a single thing to say that wouldn't come out as a muddle. How could she when all she could think about was the fact that she was now almost certain that Joe desired her as much as she desired him? If that was the case, was now the right time to ask him some of the questions that had been burning holes in the back of her mind?

Before she had time to formulate the first of them, he cleared his throat and she jumped as if she'd been shot.

'Vicky, I don't know when I last enjoyed an evening more,' he rumbled, his accent more pronounced than usual and his voice several husky notes deeper.

He was back to staring at the cloth again and in spite of the intimate lighting Vicky could see that even the tops of his ears seemed to have gone a darker colour.

'You can probably tell that I'm seriously out of practice at this sort of thing…taking a woman out, I mean.'

'I wouldn't have guessed because I haven't had much practice at being taken out myself,' she admitted in a sudden burst of equally painful honesty, while her heart turned somersaults at the thought that he'd actually implied that he saw her as a woman now, and not just a girl.

'After I lost Celia, I pretty much resigned myself to being a widower, but these last few weeks, well, you've dragged the old bear out of his cave and persuaded him to kick up his heels a bit.'

'You're not so much of an old bear,' she objected with a smile, knowing that Francine had been right. He did look years younger when he forgot himself in laughing and teasing her.

'Too old for you, though,' he stressed seriously, all trace of his former fascination with her mouth gone as completely as if she'd imagined it.

'Any why is that?' she challenged, very conscious that suddenly they were in the middle of a conversation that could affect the rest of her life.

'Well, there are eleven years between the two of

us,' he pointed out, as if that were explanation
enough.

'What does that have to do with anything?' she
retorted. 'Don't you think Francine and Andy are
happy?'

'Francine and Andy?' That had obviously thrown
him off track.

'There are more years between *their* ages than there
are between ours,' she pointed out gently. 'And I
don't think it's made the slightest bit of difference to
either of them ever since they met.'

Vicky was tempted to say more, but when she saw
the thoughtful expression on Joe's face as he looked
at her across the table, she decided to leave him time
to mull things over.

After that, although their conversation stayed low-
key right up until Joe walked her to her front door,
Vicky was very conscious of the nervous hum of anticipation settling deep inside her.

'Coffee?' she offered hopefully as she gazed up at
him from her doorstep, but he silently shook his head.
She was more than disappointed because she really
didn't want their evening to end, and she'd been so
sure that this time...

'Vicky,' he murmured, his husky voice barely
louder than the breath of wind gusting around them.
And then he was holding her in his arms and his head
was close enough to blot out the rest of the world as
he touched his lips to hers.

She'd been wrong, she realised in that fraction of
a second while her brain was still capable of rational
thought. He didn't taste of dessert or of Joe but both
together in an irresistible combination.

She could have screamed with frustration when he

suddenly tightened his hands on her shoulders and wrenched the two of them apart.

'Don't look at me like that,' he growled, dragging his fingers through his hair. He was clearly disgusted with himself for some reason, but she hadn't a clue why. 'Vicky, I'm sorry about that but—'

'I'm *not*,' she interrupted swiftly, suddenly needing to set matters straight. She never had been very good at guesswork. 'I'm not in the least bit sorry because that's what this whole evening has been leading up to, hasn't it?'

'What?' That had startled him, and by the look of his fierce frown he obviously wasn't pleased by the implication. 'You think I took you out for a meal so that I could come on to you when I brought you home?'

'No,' she said firmly. 'On the contrary. I think that in spite of some of the serious things we talked about, the two of us had a good time this evening and it just confirmed what we'd already discovered some time ago—that we're attracted to each other. What could be more natural than that you'd test the waters to see how far the attraction went? In fact, you only made one mistake.'

'A mistake? And what was that?' He was bemused now, obviously uncertain just how to take her. At least that was better than apologising, but it still left Vicky hoping she could find the words and the courage to see this conversation through to its logical conclusion. As she'd admitted in the restaurant, it wasn't as if she'd had a great deal of practice in such matters.

She drew in a shaky breath, hoping he couldn't hear the way her heart was trying to beat its way out of her chest.

'Joe, when you kiss me, you don't wait long enough for me to respond,' she whispered, reaching up to slide her fingers through the silky hair on the back of his neck and urge his head towards hers. 'Otherwise you'd *know* there's no need to apologise.'

The last word was spoken against his mouth and he took full advantage of her parted lips with a husky groan that sounded suspiciously like surrender.

Vicky was still smiling when she slid into bed and every nerve in her body was humming.

She hadn't wanted Joe to go. She would far rather have invited him into her little cottage and locked the door against the rest of the world.

Unfortunately, his will-power had been stronger than hers.

By the time they'd come up for breath she'd been completely limp in his arms, her heart exulting that he'd finally realised they felt the same way about each other.

Her celebration had been short-lived, lasting only long enough for him to open her door and see her safely inside.

'I'll see you tomorrow,' he'd said softly, and a fleeting frown had pleated his forehead as if he'd just remembered something painful. 'There are some things we need to talk about and it's too late to go into them tonight. We've both got to work tomorrow. Don't forget to lock up.'

Vicky was too excited to sleep, replaying every word, every gesture as if she were some star-struck teenager.

The phone rang and she didn't bother turning the

light on as she reached for it. Was Joe having the same trouble sleeping?

'Slut!' hissed a venomous voice in her ear, shocking her rigid as he started to rant. 'I saw you, sticking your tongues down each other's throats. You're no better than animals. Well, if that's what you like…'

Her hand was shaking so much she could hardly manage to hang up on him, and even when she did, she didn't know what to do next.

The realisation that he'd somehow managed to find out her new phone number shook her, but not as much as the realisation that he'd been out there somewhere, watching her.

Was he still out there? Would the fact that she'd hung up on him make him so angry that he'd try to break in?

She snatched up the phone again, desperate to speak to Joe, and then couldn't remember his number.

'Think, Vicky,' she muttered while the dialling tone burred in her ear. 'Calm down and think. You've got to phone someone.'

The thought of dialling the emergency services made her cringe. Just the idea of having sirens and flashing lights converge on the cottage when there was nothing but a phone call to report made her cringe.

Suddenly she remembered the WPC with the Italian name. She'd given her a number to phone, day or night, and she knew exactly where she'd put it. In her purse…right next to the card with Joe's mobile number scrawled on the back.

'Joe? Oh, thank God you're there,' she gasped when he answered on the second ring. 'It's Vicky. He rang me just a minute ago. He was watching, Joe.

Watching us while we were... He said we were like animals and if that was what I wanted...'

'Vicky!' he snapped loudly in her ear, and she suddenly realised that he'd been trying to interrupt the whole time she'd been babbling at him. 'I'm coming. Now. Did you check that your doors and windows were locked?'

'Yes. All of them,' she said, sending up a prayer of gratitude that she'd immediately followed the crime prevention officer's advice to have all the special catches fitted to each door and window.

'Leave all the lights off so he can't see you moving around, then find somewhere small and safe to hide— somewhere that no one would ever think of looking— and stay still and quiet no matter what you hear until I get there. OK?'

She nodded then realised that he couldn't see her.

'OK,' she croaked. 'Please, hurry, Joe.'

Vicky's legs were trembling when she stood up to reach for her dressing-gown, and she was doubly glad that not only was it thick enough to keep her warm but the dark blue would be less visible in the dark cottage.

Even as she sped barefoot down the narrow stairs she heard the sound of someone trying her front door, and her heart rate redoubled until it was beating so fast it was making her feel sick. She knew that the glass panels in her back door were her weakest point because the wired glass hadn't been installed yet. At least she knew that it would take any intruder some time to clear enough shards away so that they could climb through without being cut to ribbons.

Now all she had to do was find a safe hiding place,

quickly, and in a cottage this small, there weren't many.

'Think, Vicky,' she muttered again as she stood in the middle of her doll-sized sitting room. Her eyes were frantically darting from one place to the other while all the time she could hear the sound of the stalker systematically exploring every possible entrance.

All her cupboards were full, so trying to make room for herself to climb in would leave a tell-tale pile of belongings pointing to her presence. There wasn't even any room under her stairs since she'd had her washing machine installed in the alcove.

'There *isn't* anywhere,' she moaned, with panic mounting in her voice. She was cowering uselessly in the corner when the sound of breaking glass in the kitchen seemed to spur her brain into activity and she suddenly saw the ideal place…the *only* place to hide.

She barely had time to position herself, her dressing-gown pulled up over her hair to hide any betraying glimpse of the fly-away blonde strands.

'Hurry, Joe,' she breathed, wrapping her arms around herself to try to control her terrified shivers. 'Please, hurry. I need you.'

Her heart was beating like a frightened rabbit's and she was sure the sound of it was loud enough to echo off the walls. Still she could hear every sound the man made as he smashed the last of the glass out of the frame so that he could climb through.

'Vic*to*ria,' said that hated voice, and she suddenly realised that it was far too close for him to be calling her from the kitchen. He must be standing in the hallway right outside the sitting-room door.

She held her breath, desperate not to attract his attention and praying that he would search upstairs first, but a sudden click flooded the room with light.

Her eyes tight shut, she tried not to think of what he would do if he discovered her hiding place, concentrating instead on the man on his way to help her. The man she loved.

'Vic*to*ria,' he called in that same hated singsong voice that had haunted her for weeks. Then suddenly it changed to a far harder, harsher tone which was strangely familiar. 'There's no point in hiding from me because you're mine. You've always been mine.'

She was terrified by the obsessive tone and knew that it was too dangerous to move while he was still in the room with her, but she had to know who was doing this to her.

Cautiously, she turned her head until she could just peer past the edge of the dark blue fabric covering her head and caught sight of the figure standing in the middle of her sitting room.

When she recognised Grant Naismith she was so shocked that she only just stopped herself from gasping aloud.

He was a doctor, for heaven's sake, and a good, caring one if recent evidence was to be believed. She couldn't believe that many locums would have put in all the extra time he must have spent in trying to track down the cause of the epidemic of deaths in that village.

So why was he doing this to her? She barely knew the man...hadn't even recognised him until he'd reminded her that they'd worked at the same hospital before she'd returned to Edenthwaite.

'That's why I came here, you know,' he said suddenly, and she realised he was pitching his voice loud enough so she could hear it wherever she was hiding. 'When you called off your engagement to Johnson I knew it was a signal that you'd realised the truth. That you couldn't marry him because you belonged to me.'

There was a sudden splintering crash and she winced, wondering which of her childhood treasures he'd just destroyed.

'You should have waited for me,' he shouted suddenly, and there was another crash, this time heavier. 'You shouldn't have let Faraday touch you, not when you know you're mine. And you *are* mine!'

By the time she heard him leaving the room shock and lack of oxygen were making her feel quite lightheaded, but she didn't dare to draw a deep breath until she heard him go up the stairs.

By the sound of the crashes and curses she heard up there he was becoming impatient with his failure to find her, and the venom in his voice was growing more terrifying the longer she stayed hidden.

Where was Joe? Why was it taking him so long to get here?

Suddenly Vicky was afraid that she might never see him again, would never know the pleasure of spending the night with him, sharing her body as well as her heart with him.

Suddenly, the fact that the two of them had been dancing around each other for weeks seemed such a stupid waste of time, especially when it looked as if she might have come to the end of hers.

Grant was on his way back down again, more furious than ever as he continued to trash each room in turn.

Vicky was almost sobbing with fear and had to

force herself to think about something else to stop her giving her hiding place away.

Why had it taken her so long to realise what was important in her life? Why had she ever thought that the prospect of motherhood was more important than loving Joe and being with him? If she could wind back the clock to the day he'd told her he wasn't interested in having a family...but you could never wind back the clock. Once time had passed, it was gone, no matter how hard you wished.

And her time had just narrowed to the distance it would take for the ranting figure who'd just returned to her tiny sitting room to discover her and drag her out into the room. Each piece of furniture was being dragged away from the wall and upended, and he sounded as if he was standing almost close enough for her to reach out her hand and touch him when the house was suddenly filled with the banshee wail of a nearby police car.

She nearly shrieked in shock at the sheer volume. It sounded as if there were dozens of them right outside.

Don't move, whatever you hear, Joe had said, so she stayed where she was while someone with a megaphone issued demands for Grant to surrender.

She didn't know whether the police could hear his foul-mouthed defiance but she could certainly hear his frantic last-ditch efforts to find her.

She resorted to prayer again, desperate not to be used as a hostage to allow him to get away. Not now that she had the hope that she would have time to tell Joe her decision and to act on it.

She knew he still had secrets. After all, he'd said earlier tonight that they needed to talk. She had a few secrets of her own, but they were nothing that Joe couldn't take care of.

Her thoughts were shattered by a sudden noise outside the sitting-room window and then the glass exploded in all directions, raining down around her even in her hiding place.

There was an ominous hissing noise that she couldn't place, and then she caught a whiff of an acrid smell that stung her eyes and grabbed at her throat.

When Grant cursed again and began coughing uncontrollably, Vicky suddenly realised that the police must have used some sort of tear gas to disable him.

With her eyes already tightly shut and her face buried in the thick folds of her dressing-gown, she would probably fare a little better—at least until she was in no danger from the man who'd been trying to ruin her life.

There was a lot of noise going on but she was trying to ignore it, concentrating on breathing as slowly and as sparingly as possible. The last thing she wanted was to give away her hiding place before it was safe.

'Victoria Lawrence,' bellowed the man with the megaphone and she cringed, but then the voice changed.

'Vicky,' said Joe's softer, deeper voice, and her heart leapt in recognition. 'It's safe to come out now.'

For a moment she couldn't move. She'd been stuck in the same position for so long and had become so chilled in spite of the thick fabric of her dressing-gown that she was too stiff.

'Vicky, sweetheart. Can you hear me?' Joe called. Although his voice sounded slightly muffled, this time he didn't need amplification because he was right in her sitting room.

'I'm here, Joe,' she called, hoping he could hear her voice through the cuff she was holding against her face.

She pushed feebly against the wicker basket of logs that sat in the middle of the stone-built fireplace. It only slid forward a few inches but that was enough to attract Joe's attention and tell him where she was.

In seconds he was helping her out of her cramped position at the back of the fireplace and was pulling her into his arms with a wordless groan.

'Oh, Joe,' she began, but her first breath had her choking from the effects of the gas that still swirled around the room.

'Hang on and I'll get you out of here,' he ordered through his borrowed mask as he swung her up into his arms. 'There's glass everywhere and you need some fresh air.'

'Bring her this way, sir, so we can check up on her,' someone called when they emerged into the luridly lit night.

'No need,' he growled as he set her gently on her feet and stripped off the gas mask he'd donned to enter the cottage. His eyes never left her face, their expression telling her that he was almost afraid she'd disappear if he didn't hold onto her. 'I'll be taking care of her myself.'

'Joe,' she breathed as her heart began to soar, then she caught sight of movement out of the corner of her eye as a handcuffed figure was led, struggling, towards one of the police cars.

The policeman had a protective hand on Grant's head to guide him into the back of the police car when he paused to glare back at the two of them. The expression in his eyes was almost manic as he screamed at Joe, 'Leave her alone! She's mine!'

Joe bent to swing Vicky up into his arms again then strode past the various groups of emergency personnel towards his car.

'Doctor, if we could just have a word,' called a voice somewhere behind them, but he didn't even slow down.

'Tomorrow,' he growled over his shoulder, tightening his arms around her.

'This won't take long,' the police inspector insisted as he planted himself between them and Joe's car. 'I've just received some interesting information over the radio. As soon as we knew who our stalker was, we sent an officer over to his home address and he found dozens of photos plastered over the walls. Some of them seem to be earlier, but most of them were apparently taken at Dr Johnson's wedding reception.'

'The photographer!' Vicky exclaimed when she suddenly remembered what a pest the man had made of himself. How could she not have recognised him? Probably because she'd been more concerned about other things at the time. Probably because, in spite of his delusions, he'd never been important to her.

'I knew he was far too interested in taking your picture,' Joe muttered, and she wondered if he realised how possessive *he* sounded.

'If we could take your statements before you go,' the inspector suggested. 'It shouldn't take very long.'

'You can take all your statements in the morning,' Joe said firmly as he walked around the man and strode towards his car. Then he continued, for Vicky's ears alone, 'We've got a few statements of our own to make before then, and this time we're not going to put them off for another time.'

CHAPTER TEN

IN SPITE of the heating having been turned up to its highest, Vicky was still shivering when Joe pulled the car up beside the back door of his farmhouse.

'The back door's open,' she pointed out in surprise as a wide swathe of light spread out towards the car.

'My fault,' he admitted gruffly. 'I was in too much of a hurry to bother closing it.'

Vicky shuddered.

With just those few words he had painted an all-too-vivid picture of the last...what was it? Thirty minutes? An hour? She really had no idea because time had lost all its meaning when she'd huddled in the sooty blackness, waiting for discovery.

'You're freezing,' he exclaimed, and hurried round to her side of the car. She didn't bother to correct him, grateful for the warm strength of his arms around her as he once again swung her out of the car and carried her into the brightly lit kitchen.

This time he paused long enough to push the door closed, and they both heard the catch of the lock click firmly home.

He hesitated for a moment, his eyes sweeping over what he could see of her in a very clinical assessment, then strode straight through and out into the hallway.

'You need a bath,' he said bluntly, and she giggled nervously.

'That bad, am I?' She could just imagine what she must look like, having spent however long it had been

crouched in the soot at the back of her fireplace in
the shadow of the log basket.

He groaned briefly as he set her on her feet and
she suddenly remembered his injured shoulder.

'You shouldn't have carried me,' she said, guilt-
struck that she might have damaged it again just for
the wonderfully secure feeling of being carried in his
arms. 'I could have walked, you know.'

'I know,' he said softly, huskily. 'But I needed to
hold you—to make sure that you were real and you
were safe.'

'Joe,' she breathed, unable to say any more when
she saw the tormented expression in his eyes. How
could she doubt that everything was going to end happily when she could see how much he'd worried
about her, how glad he was that she was out of danger?

When she thought he would lean forward to kiss
her he actually stepped back to reach for the taps,
adjusting the temperature of the water before switching it to the shower.

'There's shampoo and soap on the edge of the bath
and plenty of warm towels on the heated rail,' he said
briskly. 'I'll just go and find you something to
wear...'

'Joe.' Vicky touched his arm as he would have left
the room, and he stopped in his tracks as though she'd
nailed his feet to the floor. 'Don't go,' she whispered,
taking the single step to bring her close enough to
lean against him, her body against the lean length of
his back.

Now that she'd finally made her decision, she wondered just what had been so hard. Joe was the other
half of her soul, whether they ever had children or

not. Even the formality of marriage seemed unimportant after the trauma of the last few hours.

'Vicky, you don't need to be afraid,' he promised earnestly, turning back towards her and capturing her chilly hands in his much larger, warmer ones. 'With any luck, Naismith isn't going to be seeing anything but iron bars for some time.'

'I'm not afraid of Naismith,' she assured him solemnly as she looked up into eyes that gleamed with golden streaks against the green. 'I just need to have you near me, to know I'm not going to lose you. Will you…will you share the shower with me?'

She could see from the arrested expression on his face that she'd startled him but then his eyes darkened and heated.

'Vicky, we can't… I can't share a shower with you without wanting to… There are things we need to talk about before we…'

'Joe.' She silenced him with a fingertip on the soft fullness of his mouth. 'I know there are things we need to discuss, secrets that we need to uncover, but they really don't matter at the moment. We can talk about them later, can't we?'

She was nervous as her hands went to the tie of her dressing-gown because she'd never done anything this bold before, had never even undressed in front of a man. But deep down she knew that this was right for both of them.

'Vicky!' he groaned when the heavy weight of the thick fabric pulled it off her shoulders to drop around her feet. The oversized T-shirt underneath it was stretched and misshapen with age and thin from too many washings and it drooped sadly over one shoul-

der, but from the avid expression in Joe's eyes it
could have been made of the finest silk.

She saw the effort it took to drag his eyes up from
the twin points of evidence of her body's arousal, and
when she met his eyes again she knew her long wait
was over.

'Let me help you,' she offered, reaching for the
buttons on the front of the black shirt she'd admired
earlier in the evening, then sent a flirtatious glance up
at him. 'You might need to rest your shoulder for
later.'

'Shoulder? What shoulder?' he retorted as he
reached for the hem of her T-shirt and stripped it off
over her head in one smooth move. 'Oh, Vicky,' he
groaned when he saw her naked for the first time.

She resisted the initial impulse to cover herself,
squaring her shoulders to stand proudly in front of
him. She only realised what her posture did to the
prominence of her breasts when he groaned aloud and
reached out towards them, only hesitating at the very
last moment.

'Shower,' he said firmly, resisting the temptation
to touch—much to her disappointment.

'Shower *together*,' she retorted equally firmly, and
reached for the waistband of his chinos.

With both of them helping, it took longer than ever
to take Joe's clothes off but finally they were standing
under the blessed warmth of the pelting spray.

Vicky had been longing to get her hands on his
body for so long and now that she had her chance she
was almost too hesitant to take advantage of it.

In the end, simple greed had her reaching for the
soap and smoothing it across the firm swells of his
muscular chest, a greed to explore that wouldn't be

satisfied until she'd investigated every inch. Even then, she couldn't foresee a day when she wouldn't want to touch him, to love him, to possess him.

'Enough!' Joe groaned when her hands began to follow the trail of soap bubbles down past his navel and beyond. 'My turn.' And he proceeded to tease and tantalise her until she burned with impatience.

'Please, Joe. Please,' she panted, pressing eager kisses over his face and nipping experimentally at his chest. She didn't really know what she wanted but her body was telling her it wanted it *now*.

As if he'd reached the end of his patience too, Joe turned the taps off and climbed out to retrieve the towels.

Vicky caught her first full-length sight of his body and decided towels were an unnecessary distraction.

'Please, Joe,' she repeated as she stepped out of the bath and totally ignored the thick warm fabric to walk straight into his arms.

'Please,' she whispered again with her fingers tangled in the wet hair on the back of his head, but this time the word was spoken against his lips.

He returned her kisses with increasing fervour for several heart-stopping moments then wrenched his mouth away to press his forehead against hers and trap her hands against his chest with his own.

'Are you sure, Vicky?' he demanded unsteadily, his breathing as laboured as if he'd run a marathon and his heart pounding beneath her palm.

'Oh, yes, Joe,' she said fervently, retrieving one hand and cupping it lovingly along his lean jaw to run a teasing thumb over his lower lip. 'I've never been more sure of anything in my life.'

He took her at her word, leading her into his bed-

room to find the bed still rumpled from his sudden
exit when he'd gone to her rescue.

'I should make the bed,' he began distractedly, and
she chuckled, suddenly feeling far less nervous when
she realised he was also edgy.

'Why bother?' she said as she wrapped her arms
around him. 'We're only going to wreck it in a minute.'

He chuckled too, and swooped to kiss her again.

'Sensible lady,' he whispered as he joined her in
the middle of the tangled covers.

He drew in a sharp breath of discomfort when he
slid over her and tried to support his weight on his
elbows, and Vicky suffered a swift pang of guilt.

'You've injured your shoulder again, carrying me
around,' she accused, and pressed him back against
the covers to examine the joint with careful fingers.

He bore her ministrations in relative silence for
several seconds before he interrupted.

'There are other areas that would welcome your
attention more,' he suggested, his voice rough with
raw desire as he guided her to straddle his body.

Vicky took a startled breath and blinked down at
him. With her lack of experience this wasn't exactly
how she'd envisioned this scene, but that didn't mean
that she wasn't willing to experiment.

And the experiment was going far better than she
could ever have imagined right up until the moment
that she joined their bodies together for the first time
and couldn't help the startled mew of surprise.

'Vicky?' Joe grabbed her around her waist to stop
her moving. 'You're a virgin?'

'Not any more,' she said with a chuckle that
sounded decidedly earthy even in the masculine con-

fines of his bedroom. She gave an experimental wriggle and when he groaned in response she moved a little more, delighted to discover how good…how *right* it felt to be joined to him this way.

'Help me,' she whispered when she realised she had no idea what to do to please him. 'Teach me.'

'Teach you what?' His voice was so deep it was almost guttural and his eyes were burning into her wherever they touched.

'Everything,' she said with an uncertain shrug. 'Everything that I chose to ignore in favour of twenty years of non-stop education.'

He gave a hoarse chuckle as he reached up to stroke the blush she could feel heating her cheek. 'I don't know if I can manage *everything* in one night, but I'll do my best.'

The annoying insistence of an alarm clock dragged Vicky out of an exhausted sleep, but when she realised that she was firmly wrapped in Joe's arms, she didn't mind.

She could get used to this in a hurry, she thought happily. In fact, she couldn't imagine waking up any other way for the rest of her life.

She slid slowly around, trying not to wake him, but once she could see his face she realised that it had been a wasted effort. He looked as if he'd been awake for some time.

'Good morning,' she murmured with a hesitant smile, surprised that she could still feel any shyness with him after what had happened between them during the long hours of the night.

'Good morning,' he said, but there was no smile to accompany it.

Vicky felt a trickle of unease snake its way between her shoulder-blades and raise all the hairs on the back of her neck. How could he *not* smile this morning?

'What's wrong, Joe?' she asked bluntly, her fear of imminent death last night having convinced her that nothing was gained by hiding secrets until a more 'convenient' time.

Her biggest secret was now a thing of the past and, far from her innocence discouraging Joe, he had actually seemed to spend their night together revelling in the role of teacher.

That was last night. This morning seemed to be a different matter.

There was a definite wariness in his eyes mixed with that old pain which she'd hoped to banish when they finally came together.

'We should have talked first,' he said finally, wearily. 'Even though this became inevitable, there were things I should have explained before we...'

He seemed lost for words but Vicky's growing irritation was supplying a few he could choose from.

'Before we made love?' she suggested first. 'Before we had sex?' was her second offering.

'Vicky, don't,' he said sadly. 'This was why I tried so hard to keep some distance between us. Because I knew that it would come to this. Because it *had* to.'

'Because it *had* to?' she repeated when she shrugged off his hand. She wriggled round until she could sit up in the bed with the coffee-and-cream-coloured duvet tucked up under her arms. 'Why does it have to end like this when we've only just started? Why does it have to end at all?'

Joe closed his eyes as if her words brought him pain. 'Because I can't give you what you want, Vicky.

Surely you can see that.' He made a wordless sound of impatience as though he was having difficulty finding the words he wanted. 'Because I was attracted to you, because I wanted you, I let myself be persuaded that it could work, that I could live in your sunshine for a while. But in the cold light of day there are obviously too many things against us.'

'Too many things against us?' she repeated angrily. 'They can't be that obvious if I can't see any of them. Name one.'

'The difference in our ages, for a start,' he muttered unhappily, leaning against the headboard and looking almost like a wary animal being backed into a corner. 'I'm too old for you, Vicky. You've got your whole life ahead of you.'

'We demolished that argument in the restaurant, remember? And you certainly weren't too old for me last night,' she pointed out pertly, hiding her hurt under a veneer of audacity. 'If that was an example of you being too old for me then all I can say is I'm glad I didn't meet you when you were any younger— I'd probably have died of pleasure.'

'Vicky, don't,' he said softly, and she had to bite her lip to control the tears that burned her eyes. 'I'm too old for you because I can't do this again. You're young and you've only had one brush with disappointment. You'll soon find a man who's ready and willing to give you everything you deserve. I've already been there and done it and it nearly killed me.'

He was being utterly serious and she couldn't treat his words any other way, no matter how much she disagreed with them.

'So you're afraid to try again?' she said bluntly,

and saw him wince at the words before he gave a wearily accepting nod.

'Afraid to risk that sort of pain again,' he corrected bleakly. 'Celia and I had it all. We shared a profession and many of the same ideals and we had a wonderful marriage, and when we'd both finished our training we decided to start our family.'

The words sounded as if they were being wrenched out of him one by one, and she hardly dared blink in case she missed any of them. This was the heart of who he was, what he'd become, and she needed to know all of it if she was going to be able to fight against it for her own happiness.

For a moment he seemed to be lost in the darkness of his memories but then he dragged himself back to continue.

'After she became pregnant she was scanned at twelve weeks and again at twenty because she wasn't absolutely certain of her dates. The second scan identified an intrauterine mass.'

'Oh, Joe,' Vicky breathed, sharing his terror and his pain all these years later.

'The consultant recommended immediate termination so the treatment would have the best chance of long-term success. Celia couldn't bear the idea of killing our baby and decided to take a gamble.' He drew in a harsh breath that told her how hard-won his control was. 'The gamble didn't pay off...for either of them.'

What could she say? There were no words that could lessen the pain of losing his wife and child in one fell swoop, and she ached for him. It was all too easy to see why he'd been so wound up over

Francine's refusal to let him help her. It must have seemed like a bad case of *déjà vu*.

But *he* was still alive and she loved him enough to fight for him. If that meant pointing out some uncomfortable facts…

'So you made the decision to retreat into your own little haven—a place of safety where the pain couldn't reach you any more.'

Joe glanced at her sharply, a wary animal sensing danger from an unexpected quarter as she continued.

'You live your life like a monk, barely communicating with the rest of the world unless they visit you as a patient, and when you're not on duty you shut yourself up in this house where the world can't reach you.'

'That's not quite—'

Vicky rode right over him, not allowing his squirming ego to derail her when she was so close to the punch-line.

'You know…' she said thoughtfully, gazing deliberately around the beautiful proportions of the room and contemplating just how welcoming it could look with a lick of paint and some full-length curtains, how right the whole house was for a rowdy, loving family. 'You know, Joe, cemeteries do the same job of protecting people, but they usually wait until they're dead before they're buried.'

Out of the corner of her eye she saw the whitened knuckles that told her the jibe had gone home.

She didn't want to hurt him—he'd been hurt enough for one lifetime—but she did want to make him look at his decisions again, especially if it meant that he would also look at the possibility of a long-term relationship with her.

'You don't know what it was like,' he growled defensively.

'I know I don't,' she admitted honestly. 'And I hope I never do. But that doesn't mean that I want to shut myself up in a box just in case it happens. What about all the years you had with Celia before she fell ill? Were they good? Were you happy?'

'Of course they were good,' he retorted, too easily for her liking, the green imp of jealousy raising its head. 'Why do you think I was so devastated when—'

'So you don't wish you'd never met her?' she interrupted swiftly.

'God, no!' he exclaimed. 'She was sweet and loving and supportive. I wouldn't have missed that for…'

There must have been something other than jealousy in her face that halted his litany of praise and left him with a stunned expression as the penny dropped.

He dropped his head back against the headboard with a resounding thud as he groaned his recognition.

'Touché,' he said wryly, and heaved a great sigh.

'You had good years with her before you lost her and you've probably still got a thousand happy memories,' she said softly, one hand coming to rest on the arm lying closest to her. 'But when she died you concentrated on the pain of losing her rather than remembering and celebrating all the reasons why you'd loved her in the first place.'

'For someone so innocent, you're very wise,' he said with a hint of amazement. 'Are you sure you're not older than twenty-six?'

'I'm getting older by the minute,' she pointed out. 'By the time you're ninety-one, I'll be eighty.'

Vicky watched the smile leach off his face and the

hand of fear clenched tightly around her heart. Surely he wasn't going to come up with any more objections.

'Joe, can I tell you a secret?' she asked unsteadily, knowing that sometimes it hurt less to get something over with rather than dragging it out—at least, that's what she'd told her patients when she'd taken a dressing-off.

She certainly wasn't going to leave this room until she'd exhausted all her ammunition, even if she blew her own boat out of the water.

'Another secret?' he corrected, reminding her that he'd only discovered the secret of her virginity when they'd reached the point of no return.

'My last secret,' she reassured him. 'It's a fairly innocent one in the scheme of world affairs but fairly important to me.'

'And to me?'

'That would depend on your reaction to it, I suppose,' she said nervously, wishing now that she'd had the courage to say it at some time during the night when they'd been in the throes of passion. It was very much harder in the cold light of day while they sat stiffly under the duvet on opposite edges of the bed.

'I've got a secret, too,' he admitted, turning his hand over to thread his fingers between hers. 'In fact, a couple of them. Would you rather I went first?'

The change in Joe's voice and attitude in the last few minutes was fascinating. It was almost as if he'd had a huge weight lifted off him so that he could emerge from the imprisoning darkness.

Vicky was so busy absorbing the differences that she meekly nodded her head.

'Well, I'm hoping the first secret is similar to yours,' he began, lifting her hand to his lips and press-

ing a kiss to it before he declared, 'I love you, Vicky
Lawrence. You've brought the sunshine back into my
life.'

'Oh,' Vicky gasped in shock. Whatever she'd been
expecting, it hadn't been *that*. 'Oh, Joe, I love you,
too!' she exclaimed in delight, squeaking in surprise
when he suddenly pulled her across the gaping void
between them and into his arms.

After a night spent eagerly learning everything he
had taught her, desire was swift to ignite, needing
little more than kisses and gentle caresses to set the
flames burning higher. At this rate, conflagration was
only a short journey away.

In spite of the deepening pleasure, something at the
back of her mind wouldn't let go and eventually
Vicky had to turn her head away to break the kiss.

'Joe? You said you had a couple of secrets,' she
reminded him, with a frown pleating her forehead as
she gazed up into the lean perfection of his face.

'I had a feeling you weren't going to let that go,'
he said with a wry smile. 'You've got the sort of brain
that picks up on details and worries them to death
until you've got an answer.'

'Oh, but—'

'That's definitely not a criticism, Vicky. It's a special gift and it's probably why you're such a good
nurse. The patients certainly appreciate your attention
to detail.'

'I don't really do anything different from… Hey!
That was a neat trick,' she exclaimed wryly, 'but I'm
not letting you sidetrack me. What *was* the second
secret?'

'Ah! Foiled!' He grinned and the expression
reached all the way to his eyes. 'Actually, that's a

fairly innocent secret in its own way,' he said as he stroked a gentle hand down her side then curved it around until it came to rest in the hollow curve of her slender stomach in the cradle between her hips. 'It's just that for all the times we made love last night we didn't take any precautions against pregnancy, and I was hoping that if you *were* pregnant I'd be able to persuade you to marry me.'

Vicky couldn't help chuckling, remembering some very similar thoughts she'd had at about the same time.

'You never know,' she said with a smile. 'If you were to ask me, I might even agree to marry you *before* we know whether I'm pregnant. A honeymoon would probably be much more enjoyable if the bride isn't suffering from morning sickness.'

'Are you sure?' he said, clearly torn between delight and apprehension.

'I've been sure for a long time,' she said, and her utter certainty must have come across in her voice. 'That was the first real secret I'd ever had—that I'd fallen in love with you—and I couldn't share it with anyone except you. And you didn't want to know.'

'I do now.' Joe tilted her face up to his with a finger crooked under her chin and brushed his lips over Vicky's just the way he had the first time he'd ever kissed her. 'I want everyone to know, but most of all I want to know everything about you, and now I'm going to have the rest of my life to learn it.'

'No more secrets?' she asked, returning his kiss but spicing it with a tender brush across his lower lip with the tip of her tongue and a swift foray into the dark sweetness beyond.

He groaned and captured the intruder to engage it in an evocative duel.

'No more secrets,' he agreed. 'Not even innocent ones.'

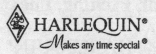

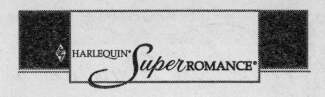

...there's more to the story!

Superromance.
A *big* satisfying read about unforgettable
characters. Each month we offer *six* very different
stories that range from family drama to adventure
and mystery, from highly emotional stories to
romantic comedies—and much more! Stories
about people you'll believe in and care about.
Stories too compelling to put down....

Our authors are among today's *best* romance
writers. You'll find familiar names and talented
newcomers. Many of them are award winners—
and you'll see why!

If you want the biggest and best
in romance fiction, you'll get it
from Superromance!

Emotional, Exciting, Unexpected...

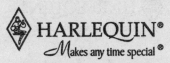

HARLEQUIN®
INTRIGUE

WE'LL LEAVE YOU BREATHLESS!

If you've been looking for thrilling tales of
contemporary passion and sensuous love stories
with taut, edge-of-the-seat suspense—then
you'll love Harlequin Intrigue!

Every month, you'll meet four new heroes
who are guaranteed to make your spine tingle
and your pulse pound. With them you'll enter
into the exciting world of Harlequin Intrigue—
where your life is on the line
and so is your heart!

THAT'S INTRIGUE—
ROMANTIC SUSPENSE
AT ITS BEST!

HARLEQUIN®
Makes any time special ®

Harlequin®
Historical

From rugged lawmen and
valiant knights to defiant heiresses
and spirited frontierswomen,
Harlequin Historicals will
capture your imagination with
their dramatic scope, passion
and adventure.

Harlequin Historicals . . .
they're too good to miss!

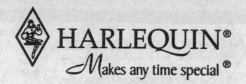

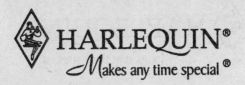

HARLEQUIN®
Makes any time special ®

AMERICAN *Romance*	Upbeat, All-American Romances

Duets™ — Romantic Comedy

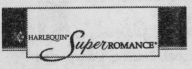

Harlequin® Historical — Historical, Romantic Adventure

HARLEQUIN®
INTRIGUE — Romantic Suspense

Harlequin Romance ® — Capturing the World You Dream Of

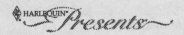

HARLEQUIN® *Presents* — Seduction and passion guaranteed

HARLEQUIN® *Super*ROMANCE® — Emotional, Exciting, Unexpected

HARLEQUIN® *Temptation.* — Sassy, Sexy, Seductive!

HDIR2